"Megh

Grey removed his horn-rimmed glasses, tucked them inside his jacket pocket and stared up at her.

Her eyelids drifted closed as embarrassment burned through her. "Pecan pie is the special of the month."

"I don't give a damn about the pie." He smiled apologetically and added softly, "But I do care about you."

"You care about me?' she echoed with disbelief.

"It's true."

She rolled her eyes. "Oh, please, spare me. You broke our date two weeks ago, and I haven't heard from you since. Believe me, Professor Carlyle, I got your message—loud and clear."

"I—

"You gave me a polite, educated brush-off in what I'm sure you felt was the kindest way possible. I can't say that I blame you. After all, you're a lofty professor, and I'm nothing more than a waitress with a love for the classics. You're educated and brilliant. I'm simply not good enough for the likes of you."

Anger flared into his eyes, sparking a bright blue fire. **"You couldn't be more wrong."**

Dear Reader,

Welcome to Silhouette—experience the magic of the wonderful world where two people fall in love. Meet heroines who will make you cheer for their happiness, and heroes (be they the boy next door or a handsome, mysterious stranger) who will win your heart. Silhouette Romance reflects the magic of love—sweeping you away with books that will make you laugh and cry, heartwarming, poignant stories that will move you time and time again.

In the coming months we're publishing romances by many of your all-time favorites, such as Diana Palmer, Brittany Young, Sondra Stanford and Annette Broadrick. Your response to these authors and our other Silhouette Romance authors has served as a touchstone for us, and we're pleased to bring you more books with Silhouette's distinctive medley of charm, wit and—above all—*romance*.

I hope you enjoy this book and the many stories to come. Experience the magic!

Sincerely,

Tara Hughes
Senior Editor
Silhouette Books

DEBBIE MACOMBER

The Way to a Man's Heart

Silhouette Romance

Published by Silhouette Books New York

America's Publisher of Contemporary Romance

To Shirley Sanders,
a special friend and my sister in Christ

SILHOUETTE BOOKS
300 E. 42nd St., New York, N.Y. 10017

ISBN: 0-373-08671-7

First Silhouette Books printing September 1989

Printed in the U.S.A.

Books by Debbie Macomber

Silhouette Romance

That Wintry Feeling #316
Promise Me Forever #341
Adam's Image #349
The Trouble with Caasi #379
A Friend or Two #392
Christmas Masquerade #405
Shadow Chasing #415
Yesterday's Hero #426
Laughter in the Rain #437
Jury of His Peers #449
Yesterday Once More #461
Friends—And Then Some #474
Sugar and Spice #494
No Competition #512
Love 'n' Marriage #522
Mail-Order Bride #539
*Cindy and the Prince #555
*Some Kind of Wonderful #567
*Almost Paradise #579
Any Sunday #603
Almost an Angel #629
The Way to a Man's Heart #671

* Legendary Lovers trilogy

Silhouette Special Edition

Starlight #128
Borrowed Dreams #241
Reflections of Yesterday #284
White Lace and Promises #322
All Things Considered #392
The Playboy and the Widow #482
Navy Wife #494
Navy Blues #518
For All My Tomorrows #530

Silhouette Christmas Stories 1986

"Let It Snow"

DEBBIE MACOMBER

hails from the state of Washington. As a busy wife and mother of four, she strives to keep her family healthy and happy. As the prolific author of dozens of best-selling romance novels, she strives to keep her readers happy with each new book she writes.

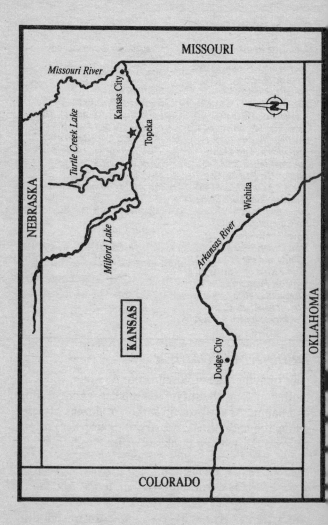

Chapter One

Are you ready to order?'' Meghan O'Day asked the man with the horn-rimmed glasses who was sitting in the booth beside the window. The gentleman was busily reading. Meghan withdrew the small tablet from inside her starched apron pocket and patiently waited for his response.

At her question, the reader's gaze reluctantly left the page of his book and bounced against her briefly. "The chicken potpie sounds good."

"Rose's potpies are excellent," Meghan said with a congenial smile. She noted that even before she'd finished writing down his order, the man had returned his attention to his reading. She grinned, not offended by his lack of notice. Some customers were chatty and openly friendly, while others preferred to keep to themselves. Meghan didn't mind. It was her job to make sure the clientele were served promptly and their needs seen to efficiently. Since Meghan was an avid reader herself, she didn't fault this gentleman for being more interested in his book than in ordering his meal.

Currently only a handful of customers dotted the diner, and the chicken-potpie order was up within a few short minutes. The reader, with his nose buried between the pages of his book, barely looked up when Meghan delivered his food.

"Is there anything more I can get for you?" she asked, automatically refilling his coffee cup.

"Nothing, thanks."

As she moved to turn away, Meghan noted that it was Geoffrey Chaucer's *Canterbury Tales*, that had captured his attention so completely. Excitement surged through her bloodstream.

Meghan herself was a devoted lover of classical literature. She set the glass coffeepot on the table and gave the reader a second look. Not bad. In fact he was downright attractive.

He glanced up at her expectantly. The only thing Meghan could do was explain. "I... Chaucer is one of my favorites."

"Mine, too." A slow, endearing smile eased across his mouth. He glanced down at the page and read in a clear, strong voice: "'Bifel that in that seson on a day, in southwerk at the Tabard as I lay—'"

"'—Redy to wenden on my pilgrimage to Canterbury with ful devout corage,'" Meghan finished reverently.

His face revealed his surprise. If she hadn't earned his attention before, she received it full force now. "You know Chaucer?"

Meghan felt a little silly and shook her head. "Not personally." Her fellow Chaucer fan didn't so much as crack a smile at her attempt at a joke. To her way of thinking, he was much too young to take life so seriously; but then she was only a waitress, not a psychologist.

"You're obviously familiar with his works." He frowned slightly and studied her as though he should be expected to recognize her and didn't.

"I've read it so many times that I've managed to memorize small portions of it. I guess you could say that Chaucer and I have a nodding acquaintance."

He chuckled at that, and planted his elbows on the table, grinning up her her. "So you enjoy reading Middle English?"

"I'll confess it was difficult going at first," she said, feeling mildly guilty for interrupting his meal, "but I stuck it out and I'm glad I did. Frankly, when I read it aloud the first time, it sounded a whole lot like Swedish to me."

A full smile courted the edges of his mouth, as if he found her insights a bit irreverent, but interesting.

A second volume rested on the seat beside him. He picked it up and ran his hand respectfully down its spine. "If you enjoy Chaucer, then you're probably a fan of Edmund Spenser, as well."

She noted that he was holding a well-read volume of *The Faerie Queene*. He continued to look at her expectantly, awaiting her reply. Feeling a bit chagrined, Meghan regretfully shook her head.

"You don't like Spenser?"

"Isn't he the one who wanted to write twelve books, each one celebrating a different knightly virtue?"

The reader nodded. "He only completed six."

"Actually, I don't think anyone minded." As far as Meghan was concerned, Spenser was a prime candidate for intensive counseling, but she couldn't very well tell her customer that. "I didn't mean to insult your tastes," she added quickly, not wanting to offend him.

The man reached for his fork, all the while studying her as if he were trying to place her. "Do I know you?"

Meghan shook her head. "Not unless you eat at Rose's Diner regularly, and I don't remember seeing you before tonight."

"This is the first time I've been here, although I've heard for years that Rose bakes the best pies in Wichita. Generally I'm not in this neighborhood." Still he continued to stare without the merest hint of apology.

"Rose will be pleased to hear that." Feeling a little foolish for lingering so long, Meghan picked up the coffeepot and took a step back. "Enjoy your meal."

"Thank you, I will." He continued to observe Meghan as she turned and headed toward the service counter. Even then, she felt his gaze.

Sherry Caldwell, the assistant manager, joined her there.

"Who's the hunk you were just talking to?"

"I don't know. He came in about twenty minutes ago, started reading Chaucer and ordered chicken potpie."

"He's cute, don't you think?" Sherry asked, eyeing him inquisitively. The assistant manager was a grandmother, but still young enough to appreciate a good-looking man when she saw one.

Meghan didn't think twice about nodding. There wasn't any doubt in her mind that this man was attractive. Everything about him appealed to her, especially his choice of reading material. Although he was sitting, Meghan could tell he was well over six feet. His dark hair was thick, cut short, and styled in a manner that gave him a distinguished air. He wasn't openly friendly, but he wasn't aloof, either. He was more of an introvert, she decided; distinguished and professional, too. Those traits wouldn't normally appeal to her, but they did in him—strongly.

From what she'd noticed, he seemed to be physically fit, but she couldn't picture him gliding down ski slopes or lifting weights. In fact, he didn't look like someone who cared much about muscle tone. He was dressed casually now, but something about him suggested he was more at home in three-piece suits and stiffly starched collars than the slacks and sweater he was wearing now.

"He's not the kind of guy one would expect to come in here, is he?" Sherry pressed.

Meghan shrugged. "I guess not, but we get all types."

Sherry chuckled. "Tell me about it, kiddo!"

The following evening, Meghan kept looking for the man who loved the literary classics, chiding herself for even expecting him to return. It wasn't like her to feel so strongly about a stranger, especially one whom she'd only talked to once. All day she thought about the handsome man who knew and loved Chaucer as she did. She would like to know him better, and wondered if he felt the same way about her.

Just when the dinner rush had started to lull, Sherry strolled past her and muttered under her breath, "He's back."

Meghan's co-worker made it sound as if an FBI agent had just stepped into the diner and was preparing to consort with the KGB. Meghan was carrying three plates of chicken-fried steak, and daring not to hope, she paused to ask, "Who's back?"

Sherry rolled her eyes. "The good-looking guy from last night. Remember?"

"I can't say that I do." Meghan preferred to play dumb, being unwilling to let her friend know how much she'd thought about seeing "the reader" again.

"The chicken potpie from last night," Sherry returned, obviously frustrated. "The one you've been watching for all night, so don't try to fool me!"

"Chicken potpie?" Meghan repeated, continuing the pretense and doing a poor job of it. "Oh, you mean the guy who was reading Chaucer?"

"Right," Sherry teased. "Well, he obviously remembered *you*. He requested your section." Sherry wiggled her finely penciled brows up and down several times.

"He did?" By now Meghan's heart was doing cartwheels.

"That's what I just finished saying."

Meghan wasn't willing to put a lot of stock in this. "I don't suppose it occurred to that romantic heart of yours to assume he was pleased with the food and the service?"

"I'm sure he was," Sherry returned, trying to suppress a smile, and failing. "But I think he's far more interested in seeing you again. After all, he could order the same cooking from any one of us."

Meghan discounted Sherry's reasoning with a soft shrug, feeling disinclined to accept anything more than the fact the handsome man who read Chaucer was back.

"Go get him, tiger," Sherry teased. "He's ripe for the pickin'."

Meghan delivered the chicken-fried steaks and re-filled coffee cups before approaching "the reader's" booth. Once again, his nose was deep in a well-worn leather volume.

"Good evening," she greeted, striving to sound friendly but not overly so—it wouldn't do to let him know how pleased she was to see him again. "You're back."

He closed the book and looked up at her. "I was in the neighborhood and decided to stop in."

"I'm glad you did." Her fingers tightened around the handle of the coffeepot. "I enjoyed our conversation last night."

"I did, too. Very much." His sober gaze continued to study her with undisguised admiration.

Meghan could tell that this man was earnest and serious. He wasn't the type to openly flirt or lead a woman on; in fact he seemed almost uncomfortable. This evening he was wearing a suit and tie and looked more dignified than ever. He was the only man in the entire diner wearing anything so formal.

He set the volume aside and looked up eagerly, reading her name tag. "It's good to see you again, Meghan."

"Thank you...and you too, of course." She set the coffeepot down, pulled her pad from the pink apron and held her pen poised, ready to write down his choice.

Instead of ordering, he held out his hand to her. "I'm Grey Carlyle."

She gave him hers and he grasped it in a firm hand-shake. Meghan had trouble pulling her gaze from his;

his eyes were a mesmerizing shade of blue that reminded her of a midsummer Kansas sky.

"I'm pleased to meet you, Meghan—"

"O'Day," she filled in. "It's Irish," she mumbled, instantly wanting to kick herself for stating something so obvious. If her name wasn't enough of a giveaway, her bright auburn hair and deep blue eyes should have been.

Suddenly there didn't seem to be anything more to say. Grey glanced at the pad in her hand and announced, "I'll order the special—whatever it is."

"Chicken-fried steak," Meghan told him eagerly.

"That sounds just fine."

Meghan took her time writing it down, wanting to linger and get to know him better. Instead she asked him, "Would you like soup or salad with your meal?"

"Salad."

She made a note of that. "What kind of dressing?"

He mulled this over as though it were important enough to involve national security. "Blue cheese, if you have it."

"We do." If they didn't she would stir up a batch herself.

"I don't suppose you've read Milton?" He turned over the book on the tabletop and showed her the cover.

Meghan held the order pad against her breast and smiled down on him. "I loved *Paradise Lost* and *Lycidas*, but the whole time I was reading his works I had the impression he was trying to get one up on Dante." The minute the words were out, Meghan wanted to jerk them back. She could feel the color sweep into her cheeks, and it was on the tip of her tongue to tell him she hadn't meant that.

The faint quiver of a smile started at the corners of his full mouth. "'Get one up on Dante'—I never thought of it quite like that before," he murmured. "But actually, you could be right."

A bell chimed softly in the background, reminding Meghan that one of her orders was ready and there were other customers who expected to be served. "I'd better get back to work," she said reluctantly. "I'll have your salad for you in just a minute."

"Before you go," he said abruptly, stopping her. "I'd like to know where you attended college?"

She cast her gaze down and shrugged, feeling slightly awkward. "I haven't."

"You haven't been to university?" Surprise elevated his voice.

Meghan looped a strand of shoulder-length hair over her ear and met his confused gaze.

"Do you mean to tell me you've done all this reading on your own?"

"Is that so unusual?"

He reached for his water glass. "Frankly, yes."

"If you'll excuse me now, I really have to get back to work."

"Of course. I'm sorry for detaining you this long."

"No, don't apologize. I enjoy talking to you. It's just that—"

"I understand, Meghan. Don't worry about it."

She stepped away from the booth, feeling uneasy with him for the first time. Literature was the one love of her life—her passion. She'd started reading early English literature when nursing her mother after she'd taken a bad fall. High school had given her enough of

a taste for the classics that she'd sought out and begun to investigate major works on her own, later.
While at home, she'd had ample opportunity to explore many of the literary greats, and in a short time
had devoured volume after volume, making a whirlwind tour of six hundred years of English literature.

As Meghan headed toward the kitchen, she noticed
Grey frowning. Now that he knew she didn't have a
degree to back up her opinions, he probably wouldn't
ask her what she thought of the classics again. It
would have been better if she'd kept her thoughts to
herself than to spout them as if she knew what she was
talking about. The habit of blurting out exactly what
she was feeling was one that continually plagued her.
Grey Carlyle was a man of culture and refinement.
Her guess was that he was a doctor or an attorney, or
someone else equally distinguished. Obviously he
knew a good deal more about literature than she ever
would.

Greyson Carlyle watched Meghan move away from
the table. In fact he couldn't stop looking at her. He'd
embarrassed her when he'd started asking her about
college, and he hadn't meant to do that.

When he'd first stepped into the diner the night before, he hadn't given her more than a second glance.
It wasn't until she'd quoted Chaucer with such a deep-
rooted love that he'd so much as looked at her. Once
he *did* notice her, however, he found himself completely enthralled. It wasn't often a man could walk
into a restaurant and find a waitress as lovely and intelligent as Meghan. In fact, meeting Meghan had
been downright unexpected. He loved the way her
Irish blue eyes lit up and sparkled when she spoke of

Chaucer and Milton. She knew these men and savored their works in much the same way he appreciated their craft and keen intelligence.

The things Meghan had said utterly intrigued him, for over the years, Grey had become far too accustomed to having his own opinions spouted back at him. Rare was the student who would have told him that Middle English sounded like Swedish. He couldn't keep from smiling at the thought.

The fact was, Grey hadn't been able to stop thinking about the impudent waitress all day. Hearing her outrageous statements was like sifting through sand and discovering pieces of gold.

He'd gone home the night before and found himself chuckling just thinking about Meghan O'Day. In the middle of a lecture the following morning, he'd paused, remembering how the young woman had told him no one was sorry Spenser had only completed six of the twelve books he'd planned. He'd broken into a wide grin and had to restrain himself from bursting out laughing right there in front of his students. The freshman class had sat there staring at Grey as if they expected him to leap on top of his desk and boogie.

Grey didn't know who'd been more shocked—his students or himself. But he'd quickly composed himself and resumed the lecture.

If Grey was going to be thinking about a woman, he chided himself later, he should concentrate of someone like Dr. Pamela Riverside. His colleague had been less than subtle in letting him know she was interested. Unfortunately, Grey wasn't the least bit attracted to her.

Instead his thoughts centered on one Irish waitress with eyes warm enough to melt stone—a waitress with a heart for the classics.

He was getting old, Grey determined. It took someone like Meghan O'Day to remind him that life didn't revolve around academia and boring social functions. The world was filled with interesting people, and this waitress was one of them.

That evening, as he walked off the campus of Friends University, Grey impulsively decided to return to Rose's Diner. He would be discussing Milton with his students in the next day or two, and he longed to hear Meghan's thoughts on the seventeenth-century poet. He was certain she would have something novel to say.

"So?" Sherry asked, cornering Meghan the minute she approached the kitchen with Grey's order. "What did he want?"

Meghan stared at her friend and blinked, pretending not to understand. " 'The reader'?"

"Who else could I possibly mean?" Sherry groaned.

"He wanted the special."

"I don't want to know what he ordered! Did he tell you why he was back again?"

Meghan chewed on the corner of her bottom lip. "Not actually. He asked what I thought of Milton, though."

"Milton? Who the hell is Milton?"

Meghan smiled at her friend. "John Milton. He wrote *Paradise Lost* and *Paradise Regained* and plenty of other, lesser-known works."

"Oh, good grief," Sherry muttered. "It's those highfalutin Greeks you're always reading, isn't it? When are you going to give up reading that antiquated stuff? Wake up and smell the coffee, Meghan O'Day. This is the eighties. If you're going to get anywhere in this life you've got to start reading real writers—like...Stephen King and...Erma Bombeck." Sherry hesitated, then nodded once for emphasis. "Take Erma—now there's a woman after my own heart. She's got more to say in one newspaper column than those Greek friends of yours say in twenty or thirty pages."

"Milton was English," Meghan corrected, smiling inwardly at her friend's mild outburst.

"What's so intriguing about these dead people, anyway?"

"It's not the writer so much," Meghan said carefully, not wanting to insult her co-worker. "It's what they had to say about the things that affected their lives."

"Stephen King doesn't do that," Sherry countered. "And he's done all right for himself."

"He has, at that," Meghan agreed. It wouldn't do any good to argue with Sherry, but she wanted her to understand. "Listen to this," Meghan asked and inhaled deeply. When she spoke, her low voice was soft and well modulated. "'Know then thyself, presume not God to scan; The proper study of mankind is man.'"

Sherry was giving her an odd look. "That's Milton?"

"No. Alexander Pope. But don't the words stir your soul? Don't they reach out and take hold of your heart and make you hunger to read more?"

Sherry shook her head. "I can't say that they do."

"Oh, Sherry." Meghan sighed, defeated.

"I'm sorry, I can't help myself. That sounds like a bunch of mumbo-jumbo to me, but if that's what turns you on, I'll try not to complain."

When Meghan had finished adding salad dressing to the small bowl of lettuce and chopped tomatoes, she delivered it to Grey's table.

"Can I get you anything else before your dinner comes up?" she asked, setting the salad in front of him along with a narrow tray of soda crackers.

"Everything's fine," he replied, and looked up at her. "Listen, I'd like to apologize if I embarrassed you earlier by asking you about your college education."

"You didn't embarrass me." It *had* somewhat, but she couldn't see that telling him that would help matters. Years before, she'd yearned to go to college, dreamed of it, but circumstances had kept her home. She didn't begrudge not attending; it was part of her life and she'd accepted the fact long ago.

"I don't mean to pry," Grey said, frowning just a little, "but I'm curious why someone who loves the classics the way you do, wouldn't pursue your schooling?"

Meghan dropped her gaze. "The year I graduated from high school my mother fell down a flight of stairs and broke her hip. She needed surgery and was immobile for several months because of complications. With three younger brothers, I was needed at home. Later, after Mom had recovered, the family was strapped with huge medical bills."

"You're helping to pay those?" Grey pressed.

"They're mostly paid now, but I'm twenty-four."

"What's that got to do with anything?"

Meghan laughed lightly. "I'd be years older than the other freshmen. I wouldn't fit in."

Grey's brows drew together, forming a deep V over his eyes. Apparently he was considering something.

"I was wondering," he said, and hesitated. "I mean, you hardly know me, but there's a lecture on the poetry of Shelley and Keats at Friends University tomorrow evening that I was planning to attend. Would you care to go with me?"

Meghan stared back at him, hardly able to believe what she was hearing. This distinguished man was actually asking her out on a date.

When she didn't immediately respond, he lowered his eyes to his salad. "I realize this is rather spur-of-the-moment."

"I'd love to go," she blurted out, scarcely able to disguise her enthusiasm.

"Shall we meet here in the parking lot...say, around seven-thirty?"

"That would be fine," Meghan responded eagerly. "I'm honored that you'd even think to invite me."

"The pleasure's all mine," Grey insisted with a boyishly charming smile.

"Until tomorrow, then," she said.

"Tomorrow," he repeated.

An hour later, Grey stood beside his car, his hand on the door handle, his thoughts excited and chaotic. He'd found a kindred spirit in Meghan O'Day. The minute she'd softly quoted Chaucer to him, his heart hadn't been the same. When he heard the reason she hadn't gone on to college, Grey knew he had to ask her to the lecture. Once she'd sampled the feast of rich works to be served the following night at the university, she would be hooked. He wanted this for her.

Even if she was a few years older than the majority of
the students, he knew she'd fit right in. He could tell
her this, but it wouldn't be nearly as effective as giving her a taste of what could be in store for her behind those walls of learning.

Grey wasn't an impulsive man by nature, but when
he was with Meghan he found himself saying and
doing the most incredible things. This invitation was
just one example.

With an unexpected burst of energy, Grey tossed his
car keys into the air and deftly caught them behind his
back with his left hand. He was so stunned by the ag-
ile move that he laughed out loud.

A light snow had just begun falling when Meghan
walked toward Grey in the well-lit parking lot in front
of Rose's Diner the following evening. Snow had arrived early this year; Wichita had already been struck
by two storms and it wasn't yet Thanksgiving.

"I hope I didn't keep you waiting long," Meghan
said, strolling up to his side.

"Not at all."

He smiled down at her and the chill that had permeated Meghan's bones was suddenly gone, vanished
under the warmth in his eyes.

Grey tucked her hand into the curve of his arm. "I
think you'll enjoy this evening."

"I'm sure I will. Shelley and Keats are two of my
favorites, although I tend to like Keats better."

Grey opened the car door for her. "I find their styles
too similar to prefer one over the other."

"Oh, I agree. But I happened to read some of Shelley's letters," Meghan added conversationally, "and

I've had trouble thinking objectively about him ever since.''

"Oh?" Grey walked around the car and joined her in the front seat. "What makes you say that?"

Meghan shrugged. "His notes to his friends were full of far-out abstractions and so dreadfully philosophical. If you want my opinion, I think Shelley was stuck on himself. In fact, I've come to think of him as a big crybaby."

Grey's eyes widened. "I thought you said you liked Shelley?"

"Oh, dear," Meghan replied, expelling her breath. "I'm sorry. I've shocked you again, haven't I?"

"It's all right," he said, the frown slowly unfolding. "As it happens, Shelley is my all-time favorite and I'm having one hell of a time not defending him. You're right, though. He was big on himself. But who could blame him?"

"No one," Meghan agreed.

"You know what I like best about you, Meghan?"
She shook her head.

"You're honest, and that's a quality I greatly admire. You aren't going to tell me something just because you think I want to hear it."

Meghan cocked her head to one side and expelled a sigh. "That—fortunately or unfortunately, as the case might be—is true. I have the damned habit of blurting out whatever I'm thinking."

"I find it refreshing," he said, reaching for her hand and squeezing her fingers. "We're going to enjoy tonight. And when the lecture is finished, we'll discuss Shelley again. I have the feeling your opinion's going to change."

Grey drove across town to Friends University. Although Meghan had passed the campus several times, she'd never actually been on the grounds. As she looked around at the ivy-covered structures, her gaze filled with longing. Some day, some way, she would find a way to further her education here.

"It really is lovely here, isn't it?" she said, once they'd parked. Grey walked around and opened her car door, his impeccable manners again impressing Meghan.

"Just standing here makes me want to curtsy to all these buildings," she commented, smiling.

"Meghan," he said kindly, tucking her hand once more into the crook of his arm. "I don't understand. You so obviously love literature, you aren't going to feel out of place once you sign up for a few classes. Yes, you would be older than the majority of first-year students, but not by much."

"It's a bit more than that," she said, looking away from him.

"If you can't afford the expense surely there are scholarships you could apply for."

"Yes, I suppose I could. But I haven't."

"Why not?"

She looked away, feeling uncomfortable. "The last thing I want to do is sit in some stuffy classroom and listen to some white-haired professor," she said defensively.

"Why not?"

Grey did a good job of disguising his shock, but Meghan knew he was dismayed. It seemed that his voice tensed a little, but Meghan couldn't be certain.

"If you really must know," she said nervously, "colleges and professors frighten me."

THE WAY TO A MAN'S HEART   25

"Meghan, that's ridiculous. They're people like and you me."

"Yes, I suppose it *is* absurd, but it's the way I feel. I'm afraid a professor would look down his learned nose at me and think I'm stupid."

"Listen," he said, placing his hands on her shoulders and turning on the pathway so that he faced her squarely. "There's something you should know."

In the distance, Meghan could hear footsteps approaching them. Grey dropped his hands, apparently wanting to wait until the group had passed him.

"Evening, Professor Carlyle."

Grey twisted his head around and nodded. "Good evening, Paul."

"Professor Carlyle," Meghan muttered. "*You're* a professor?"

Chapter Two

Meghan felt the surprise splash over her, drenching her to the bone. Grey Carlyle was a university professor, specializing in English literature, no doubt! She couldn't believe how incredibly obtuse she'd been. Just looking at him, reading Chaucer and Milton in his crisp three-piece suit, precisely knotted tie and boot-camp polished shoes should have been a dead give-away. Only Meghan hadn't figured it out. Oh, no. Instead she'd danced all around him in an effort to impress him with her dazzling insights and sharp wit—all the while making a complete nincompoop of herself.

Her gaze met his and quickly lowered. "I should have guessed," she muttered, forcing a smile.

"Is my hair that white?" he coaxed. "Do I really come off as so terribly stuffy?"

His words were a teasing reminder of the things she'd recently stated about college and professors.

"You could have gone all night without repeating that," she whispered, feeling the warm color rush into her face.

"I'm sorry, but I couldn't help myself."

"You're not the least bit sorry," she countered.

Grey chuckled and rubbed the side of his jaw. "You're right. I'm not."

"I should be furious with you, letting me go on that way!" Meghan said, still not looking at him directly. If those students hadn't arrived when they did, there was no telling how much more she would have said.

"But you're not angry?"

"No," she said, releasing a pent-up sigh. "I probably should be, but I'm not." She'd done this to herself, and although she would have liked to blame Grey, she couldn't.

"I didn't know how to stop you," he admitted, frowning. "I wanted to say something—let you know before you'd embarrassed yourself. I suppose I just assumed you'd figured it out. Which was my own fault."

"That's the problem," Meghan admitted with a rueful smile. "My tongue often outdistances my mind. I get carried away and say the most absurd things and then I wonder why everyone is giving me these incredible looks."

"Friends?" Grey prompted, holding out his hand.

His look was so endearing and so tender that Meghan couldn't have resisted had she tried. From the first moment she'd noticed Grey Carlyle reading Chaucer, she'd been attracted to him. Strongly attracted. Lots of good-looking men had passed through the doors of Rose's Diner, and plenty had shown more than a casual interest in her. But this was the first time

Meghan had ever dated anyone she'd met at the restaurant after such a short acquaintance.

"Friends," Meghan agreed, slipping her hand into his. His touch was light and impersonal, and Meghan experienced a sensation of rightness about their being together. Perhaps it was best that she hadn't guessed his occupation earlier. If she had, she might not have been so candid.

They started walking toward the ivy-covered brick buildings. The pathway was lined by small green shrubs. "I wish now I'd worn my other shoes," Meghan commented casually. The one good thing about this date was that she'd cleaned out her closest while searching for the perfect outfit. After trying on anything and everything that was the least bit suitable, she'd chosen a red plaid skirt, white blouse and dark blazer, with knee-high leather boots.

Grey paused and glanced down at her feet. "Are those too tight?"

"No, especially since I've stuck my foot in my mouth a couple of times, but my other shoes are more subtle."

"Subtle?" he repeated.

"All right," she muttered. "More dignified. If I'd known I was attending this lecture with a full-fledged professor, I'd have dressed more appropriately for the occasion. But since I assumed you were just a regular, run-of-the-mill, classical literature lover, I thought the boots would do fine."

"You look wonderful just the way you are."

The open admiration in his gaze told her he was telling the truth. "It's nice of you to say so, but from here on out, it's my black patent-leather Mary Janes."

He burst out with a short laugh. The sound was robust and full but a little rusty, as though he didn't often reveal his amusement quite so readily.

Again he securely tucked her hand in the curve of his arm. "This is a prime example of what I was talking about earlier."

"What is?" Meghan wasn't sure she understood.

"Your honesty. There isn't any pretense in you, and I find that exceptionally rare these days."

Meghan was about to make a comment, when they strolled past a group of students.

"Hello, Professor Carlyle," a blond girl said eagerly and raised her hand. When Grey turned toward her, the teen smiled brightly. "I just wanted to be sure you knew I was here."

Grey nodded.

From all the smiles and raised hands directed toward Grey, Meghan guessed he was a popular professor. God knew *she* liked him! Now that was an understatement if there ever was one. But Meghan knew she would be a fool to hope that a man like Grey Carlyle would ever be romantically interested in her—and Meghan was rarely foolish. Obtuse, yes; foolish, no! She might amuse him now, but that wasn't likely to last.

Gavin Hall was only a short distance from the lot where Grey had parked his car. The auditorium was huge, and by the time they were seated near the back of the hall, it was more than a third filled.

Two men sat near the podium. The first Meghan recognized from the newspaper as Friends's president, Dr. Browning. The other man was obviously the speaker. To Meghan's way of thinking, he resembled a prune, though she chided herself for the uncharitable thought. The lecturer seemed to wear a perpetual frown, as though everything he saw greatly displeased him. Either that, or he'd recently been sucking lemons.

"There seems to be a nice turnout," Meghan commented, impressed by the number of students who appeared to have such a keen interest in Keats and Shelley.

Grey straightened the knot of his silk tie and cleared his throat. "Actually," he whispered out of the corner of his mouth, "I bribed my class."

"I beg your pardon?"

Grey didn't look particularly proud of himself. "Dr. Fulton Essary is a colleague of mine and a distinguished poet in his own right. We've had our differences over the years, but basically I value his opinions. I wanted a good showing tonight, so I told my classes that every one of my students who showed up would automatically receive an extra fifty credits toward his overall grade."

"Ah," Meghan said softly. "That was why the blond girl made a point of letting you know she was here."

"Exactly." Grey withdrew a piece of paper from the inside of his suit jacket and unfolded it as quietly as possible. As he scanned the auditorium, he started checking off names.

Within five minutes the lights dimmed and Dr. Browning approached the podium to make his introduction. Shortly afterward, Dr. Fulton Essary stepped up to the front of his audience and delivered his speech—in a dead monotone.

For one hour and five minutes Dr. Essary summarized the life and works of Percy Bysshe Shelley and

John Keats. Although Meghan admired the talents of both nineteenth-century poets and was familiar with their styles and literary accomplishments, she was eager to learn something new.

Unfortunately, nothing she could do kept her thoughts from wandering. Dr. Essary was terribly boring.

After the first half hour, Meghan started shifting in her seat, crossing and uncrossing her long legs. At forty-five minutes, she was picking imaginary lint from the lap of her skirt.

The only thing she found riveting was the fact that someone who planned to talk for this amount of time could reveal such little emotion concerning his subjects. He might as well have been lecturing about the Walt Disney characters, Mickey and Minnie Mouse. If anything in Keats's and Shelley's lives had personally touched him, Meghan would have never known it.

Once he finished there was a round of polite, restrained applause followed by what Meghan felt was a sigh of relief that rolled over the audience. The floor was opened for questions, and after an awkward beginning, one brave student stood and asked something that Meghan couldn't fully hear or understand.

Slowly Grey moved his head toward Meghan's and whispered, "What do you think?"

It was in her mind to lie to him, to tell him what he wanted to hear; but he'd claimed he admired her honesty, and she wouldn't give him anything less now. "The man's a bore."

Grey's eyes widened at the bluntness of her remark.

Meghan saw his reaction and immediately felt guilty. "I shouldn't have said that," she told him, "but I couldn't help it. I'm disappointed."

"I understand you may have found his delivery lacking, but what about content?"

Apparently the question-and-answer session was over with the one question, because just as Meghan was about to whisper her response, everyone started to stand. Happily leaping to their feet more adequately described what transpired, Meghan mused.

She supposed she wasn't the only one to notice, but it seemed to her that the hall emptied as quickly as if someone had screamed "Fire! Run for your lives!" Grey's students couldn't get out of there fast enough. Personally, she shared their enthusiasm.

Once they were outside, Grey helped her on with her coat, slipping it over her blazer, his hands lingering on her shoulders. "You were about to say something," he coaxed.

Meghan stared up at him blankly while putting on her gloves.

Burying his hands in the pockets of his thick overcoat, Grey matched his long strides to her shorter ones. "You didn't like the lecture?"

"I . . . I wouldn't exactly say that."

"You called the speaker a bore," he reminded her, frowning.

"Yes, well . . ."

"Is this another one of those times when your tongue got away with you?" he teased, but the amusement didn't quite reach his eyes.

Meghan slipped her hands inside her coat pockets, forming tight fists, uncertain how she should respond. She probably wouldn't be seeing Grey after tonight, so there wasn't any reason to pad her answer. She wasn't sure she could, anyway. After an hour and five minutes of such insipid drivel, she was having trouble holding her tongue.

"Perhaps referring to him as a bore was a bit of an exaggeration," she started, hoping to take the bite out of her blunt remark.

"So you've changed your mind." That seemed to please Grey.

"Not entirely."

His face fell. "You can't fault Dr. Essary. Honestly, Meghan, the man's a recognized genius. He's published his doctorate on Shelley and Keats. Mention the name Dr. Fulton Essary and the literary world automatically associates him with the two poets. His own published works have been compared to theirs. He's known all across America."

Meghan had never heard of him, but that wasn't saying much. Unfortunately, as far as she was concerned if someone were to mention the name Dr. Fulton Essary, her response would be a drawn-out yawn.

"I won't argue with you," she said, carefully choosing her words, "but there's no passion in the man."

"No passion? Are you saying he should have ranted and raved and pounded his fists against the podium? Is this how you think he should have delivered his lecture?"

"No—"

"Then just exactly what do you mean by passion?" Grey demanded, obviously frustrated.

"Essary compared Keats to Shakespeare for the richness and confidence of his language, and I couldn't agree with him more, but—"

"Then what's the point?"

"The point is that for all the feeling your associate relayed, Keats could have written 'Mary Had a Little Lamb.' If what he was saying was so profound—and I think it could have been—then it should have come from his heart. I didn't feel anything from this friend of yours except disdain, as though he were lowering himself to share his insights to a group of students who are constitutionally incapable of understanding Keats's and Shelley's genius. Nothing he said gripped me, because it hadn't touched him."

Grey was silent for a minute. "Don't you think you're being unnecessarily harsh?"

"Perhaps, but I don't think so," she murmured. "Ask your students what they think. I'm sure one of them will have courage enough to be honest."

"It was a mistake to have brought you here," Grey said when they reached his car, his mouth a taut line of impatience.

He was angry—furious—and doing a remarkable job of restraining himself, Meghan noted. For that matter, she wasn't particularly pleased with him, either. He'd asked her what she thought and she'd told him. It was as if he expected her to say whatever it suited him to hear. Nor was she pleased with what he seemed to be implying. He made it sound as though she couldn't possibly know enough to make an intelligent evaluation of a man as brilliant as Dr. Essary. Good heavens! Even his name was pompous-sounding! All this evening did was reinforce the fact that she would never make it as a college student. If her supposed friend thought her stupid, what would strangers think?

Ever the gentleman, Grey helped Meghan into his car, firmly closing the passenger door and walking around to the driver's side.

The ride back to Rose's was an uncomfortable one. Grey didn't say a word and neither did Meghan. The silence was so loud, she could barely hear anything else. It was in her mind to say something to ease the tension, but one look at Grey told her he wasn't in the mood to talk. Now that she thought about it, neither was she. She did feel badly, however. Grey had invited her to the lecture and she'd gone with an open mind, eager to learn; instead, she'd come away feeling depressed and sorry.

He eased his car into the restaurant parking lot and moved to turn off the engine.

"Don't," she said quickly, sadly. "There's no need for you to get out. I apologize for ruining your evening. Despite everything, I'm grateful you invited me to this lecture—I've learned some valuable lessons. But I feel badly that I've disappointed you. I wish you well, Professor Carlyle. Good evening." With that, she opened the car door and climbed out.

As she was walking away, Meghan thought she heard him call after her, but she didn't turn around—and he didn't follow her.

It was just as well.

Chapter Three

Grey couldn't remember a time when a woman had upset him more. Streetlights whizzed past him as he hurried back to Friends University, and he realized he was traveling well above the speed limit. With a sigh of impatience, he eased his foot off the gas pedal and reluctantly slowed his pace.

Grey had asked Meghan to Dr. Essary's lecture, believing she would be stimulated and challenged by the talk as well as the man. He'd liked Meghan, been attracted to her warmth and her wit; but now the taste of disillusionment filled his mouth. In the space of only a few hours, he'd discovered that although she appeared intellectually curious, she wasn't willing to listen and learn from those who clearly had more literary knowledge than she. Being a professor himself, he felt it was like a slap in the face.

His invitation had been an impulse; and every time he acted impetuously, Grey lived to regret it. This evening was an excellent example.

Meghan was a mere twenty-four-year-old with nothing more than a high-school education. She had no right to make such thoughtless statements about a man as eminent as Dr. Essary—a man who'd made a significant contribution to the world of literature. Just thinking about Meghan's comments infuriated Grey. The other man was brilliant, and she'd had the audacity to call him a bore. To worsen matters, she'd gone on to claim that Dr. Essary had revealed little emotion for his subject. Why, anyone looking at him would know differently. All right, Grey admitted, his esteemed colleague could use a few pointers on the proper method of delivering a speech of that length, but the audience wasn't a group of preschoolers with short attention spans. These were college students— adults.

What had upset Grey most, he decided, was Meghan's claim that Dr. Essary had displayed no passion. Of all the silly comments. Good Lord, just exactly what did she expect—tears, dramatic gestures, or throwing himself down in front of the audience?

Grey had delivered plenty of lectures in his career, and his style wasn't all that different from that of his associate. No one had ever faulted Grey. No one had claimed he was a bore—no one would dare!

Back at Friends University, Grey sat inside his car for several minutes while the anger worked its way through him. Rarely had he been more outraged. The indignity burned through him like a fiery blade, hotter than what Meghan's comments warranted.

"Damn!" he shouted, and slammed his hand against the steering wheel in a rare burst of emotion.

As he climbed out of the car, the lights from a coffeehouse called Second Life from across the street attracted his attention. A number of Friends students were known to hang out there. Grey started walking in the opposite direction to the faculty reception in honor of Dr. Essary, but stopped after only a few feet. Frowning, he abruptly turned around and headed toward the café.

Meghan secured the tie of her bright yellow housecoat around her narrow waist and set the teakettle on top of the burner. Her apartment near Marina Lake was small and homey, but Meghan felt little of its welcome after this evening's disaster.

To prove exactly what kind of mood she was in, she'd walked in the door and gone directly to her bedroom to reach for her yellow robe. In fact, she hadn't even bothered to undress first.

Do not pass go. Do not collect two hundred dollars.

That was the way she felt—like a loser in a board game.

She'd blown her date with Grey. It was another one of those "open mouth and insert foot" incidents. He'd asked for her honesty, and she'd told him exactly what she thought of his friend. From there, everything had quickly disintegrated. She should have known he wanted her to lie, and gone on and on about how wonderful the lecture had been. Meghan didn't know if she was that good a liar. But it was clearly what he'd wanted to hear, and she should have given it to him and saved herself some grief.

So this was to be the end of her short-but-sweet re-lationship with Grey Carlyle. Unfortunately, it would take a while to work through the regret. Knowing the way she did things, it would take her a few days to pull herself together, to dissect the evening and put the in-cident into perspective so she could learn from what had happened. At the end of this blue funk she should walk away a little wiser.

The kettle let loose with a high-pitched whistle that broke the silence of the tiny kitchen. Meghan poured the boiling water into the teapot, added the herbal leaves and left them to steep for several minutes. She was just about to pour herself a cup when there was a knock at the door.

She glanced across the living room as though she expected there was some mistake. No one could pos-sibly be coming to visit at this hour—unless, of course, it was one of her teenage brothers; but even that was unlikely this late in the evening.

"Who is it?" she asked.

"It's Grey. Could we talk a minute?"

Grey! Meghan's hands were trembling so badly she could hardly manage to twist the lock and pull open her front door. In that short time span, she didn't have a chance to school her reaction or her thoughts. The only thing she felt was an instant surge of jubilation. The smile that spread across her face came from deep within her heart. Meghan knew without even trying, there was no way to restrain the look of sheer joy that dominated her features.

"Grey," she said, stepping aside so he could enter her apartment.

He did so, standing awkwardly just inside the door. His gaze seemed to rest somewhere behind her and refused to meet her own. His expression was brooding and serious. The smile that had sprang so readily to her face quickly faded.

"I can see this is a bad time," Grey commented, once he looked directly at her and her yellow house-coat.

"No...this is fine," she replied hurriedly. "Would you like to sit down?" Embarrassed by the load of laundry that was piled on one corner of the sofa, she rushed over and scooped it up with both hands, smiled apologetically and deposited the clean clothes on the seat of the recliner.

"You look as if you were ready for bed," Grey observed, remaining standing. "Perhaps it would be better if I returned at a more convenient time."

"No, please stay." She removed the housecoat and draped it over the back of the chair that contained her laundry. "I bought this robe several years ago when my family was on vacation in Texas," she felt obliged to explain. "Whenever I'm feeling depressed or unhappy about something, I put it on and pout for a while. My mother calls it the Yellow Robe of Texas."

Grey cracked a smile at that. "You're pouting now?"

"I was, but I'm not anymore." Meghan was delighted to see him, if only to let him know how much she regretted the way their evening had gone. She wanted to tell him how she'd felt when he'd lashed out at her, which had only driven home her own point that she wasn't cut out for college-level literature courses.

"I just put on a pot of tea. Would you like some?" she offered.

"Please."

Meghan moved into the kitchen and brought down her two best china cups, along with sugar and milk, and set them on a tray. When she turned around, she discovered Grey standing behind her, looking chagrined, his hands in his pockets.

"Aren't you the least bit curious why I'm here?"

With her heart in her throat, she nodded. The last person she had ever expected to see on the other side of her door was Grey Carlyle—*Professor* Grey Carlyle. "I'm equally curious to know how you knew where I live."

"When I went back to Rose's—I hoped you'd still be there—anyway, another waitress, I think her name was Sherry, gave me your address."

Meghan should have known the assistant manager would be willing to go against company policy for Grey. Normally the information would have had to be tortured out of her co-worker.

Grey freed one hand from inside his coat pocket and jerked his splayed fingers through his hair as though he weren't particularly pleased about something. "I told her you'd left something in my car that I thought you might need. I don't usually lie, but I felt it was important we talk."

Meghan's fingers tightened around the serving tray. "I understand."

Grey took the tray from her hand and set it on the round oak table that dominated what little space there was in her cramped kitchen. With him standing so close, the area seemed all the more limited. Despite herself, Meghan lifted her gaze to his.

Grey raised his hands to the rounded curves of her shoulders and his eyes caressed hers. "I owe you an apology."

"No," she said, and shook her head, more than willing to discount his words. "I should be the one to make amends to you. I don't know what came over me, or why I felt it was necessary to be so insensitive. I'm not often so opinionated—well, I am, but I'm usually more subtle about it. If it means anything, I want you to know I felt terrible afterward."

"What you said was true," he admitted bluntly, frowning. "Dr. Essary *is* an arrogant bore. The reason I took exception to your description of him is because Essary and I are actually quite a bit alike."

"I'm sure he's a fine man of sterling character—" Meghan stopped abruptly. "I beg your pardon?" She was sure she'd misunderstood Grey. He couldn't possibly mean to suggest that he was anything like his colleague. She didn't know Grey well, but everything in her heart told her Professor Carlyle was nothing like the other man.

"After dropping you off, I drove back to the university campus. I'll admit I was angrier than I've been in a long time. I sat in my car fuming, feeling confused. I couldn't seem to put my finger on why I should be so insulted." He paused, pulled out a kitchen chair and gestured for Meghan to sit down. She did and he took the seat across from her.

"You were defending your friend, the same way he would have supported you," Meghan reassured him, silently chastising herself for her arrogant ways.

"Not true," Grey contradicted, his frown growing darker and more intense. "Fulton and I have never considered ourselves in those terms. You might even say we have a friendly rivalry going on between us."

Since they were both sitting, Meghan poured the tea, handing Grey his cup. Her fingers were far more steady now.

"Something you said, however, struck a note with me," he continued. "You suggested I ask my students what they thought. You seemed confident at least one of them would open up to me."

Meghan did vaguely remember suggesting that.

"A group of my pupils were having coffee after the lecture. I joined them and asked for their honest opinion." He hesitated, looking mildly distressed. "I asked. And by God, they gave it to me with both barrels."

Hearing that others shared her sentiments didn't cause Meghan to feel better about what had happened between her and Grey, but it helped.

While he was talking, Grey added both sugar and milk to his tea, stirring it in as though the sweetener were made of some indissoluble compound. "I took a long hard look at Fulton," Grey continued, "and what I saw was a sad reflection of myself."

"Grey, no." Her hand automatically reached for his.

"Meghan, you don't know me well enough to contradict me."

"But I do.... I realize we've only talked a few times, but you're not anything like Dr. Essary. I know it as surely as I'm convinced we're sitting here together."

He captured her fingers and squeezed lightly. "It's kind of you to say so, but unfortunately I know differently. My life has been filled with academia and its importance. In the process, I've allowed myself to become jaded toward life, forgetting the significance of what I thought were trivial matters. In the last few years, I've immersed myself in a disapproving, wet-blanket attitude.''

"I'm sure you're mistaken."

His smile was sad, his features grim. "I've laughed more with you in the past few days than I have all year. I look at Fulton, so deadpan and serious, and I recognize myself. Frankly, I don't like what I'm seeing. If you feel there's no passion in him, you're right. But there's none in me, either. It's not something I'm proud to admit. Fun is often associated with frivolity. And as a learned man—an educator—I've looked upon fun as a flaw in the character of a man.'' He studied his cup as though he expected the tea leaves to spell out what he should say next. "I owe you much more than an apology, Meghan. In only a few short days you've revealed to me something I'd been too blind to recognize until now. I want you to know I'm truly grateful.''

Meghan didn't know what to say. "I'm sure you're putting more stock than necessary in all this. The minute I met you I saw an intense, introverted man of undeniable intelligence who loved Chaucer and Milton the same way I did. I'm nothing more than a waitress at a popular diner, and you shared your love for the classics with me. If anything, that made you more appealing to me than a hundred other men.'' Meghan understood all too well the differences between them. Grey was accustomed to a refined, academic atmosphere while she was fun loving and slightly outrageous. From the moment she'd started talking to him, Meghan had recognized Grey's type. He was analytical, weighing each fact, cataloging each bit of information before acting. Impulsive actions were as foreign to him as a savings account was to her.

"What I saw was a bright, enthusiastic woman who—"

"Who doesn't know when to keep her mouth shut," Meghan finished for him.

They both laughed, and it felt good. Meghan took a sip of her tea, feeling almost light-headed. She realized it had taken a good deal of internal fortitude for Grey to come to her this way.

He glanced at his watch, arched his brows as though he were surprised by the time, and stood abruptly. "I'm sorry for interrupting what remains of your evening, but I wanted to talk to you while I still had the courage. The longer I put it off, the more difficult it would have been."

Meghan appreciated what it must have cost him to confront her, and her estimation of him, which was already high, increased a hundredfold. She didn't want him to leave, but she couldn't think of an excuse to delay him.

"I know how difficult it was for you to come by. I'm glad you did."

"I am, too." He edged his way to the front door.

Meghan's mind was racing frantically in an effort to prolong his leaving. She thought to suggest a game of Monopoly, but was certain he'd find that childish. Cards weren't likely to interest him, either.

"Thanks for the tea."

"Sure," she said with a shrug. "Any time."

His gaze fell on the yellow robe that had been carelessly draped over the recliner. A smile bounced against the corners of his mouth. "Good night, Meghan."

She went to open the door for him, but his hand at her shoulder stopped her. She turned, and his nar-

rowed gaze met hers in a lazy, caressing action. His
eyes were filled with questions, but Meghan couldn't
decipher what it was he wanted to know. A contest of
wills seemed to be waging within him as his look continued to embrace her. Meghan returned his gaze, not
understanding but wanting to help in any way she
could.

"Every time I act on impulse I regret it."

She blinked, not knowing what to make of his
comment. "Sometimes it's the only thing to do," she
murmured. "My mother always claimed I should follow my heart. That's good advice—I suggest you do
the same."

The frown left him, to be replaced by a determined
grin. "You're right. Sometimes doing what seems
natural is by far the best thing. God knows, I won't
ever regret this." With that, he lowered his head to
hers and she felt the warm brush of his mouth across
her own. He slipped his arm around her waist and
gently pulled her against him, half lifting her from the
floor. He touched the upper part of her lip with his
tongue, lightly, and moistened the outline of her
mouth.

A choppy rush of air escaped from her lips at this
subtle attack on her senses. Meghan moaned softly
and leaned into him, letting his weight absorb her
own. Then, moving her head farther back, Grey
rubbed his lips against hers, applying a gentle pressure until her mouth parted in welcome, eager for a
more thorough exploration.

Meghan shouldn't have been so surprised that he
should kiss her, but she was. She flattened her hands
against his hard chest, her fingers clenching handfuls

of his shirt as she gave herself over to the wealth of sensation that rocked through her.

It was a short kiss as kisses went; his mouth lingered over hers for only a heartbeat more and then quickly withdrew, leaving her hungering for more.

"I'd like to see you again," he said in a voice that sounded unlike his own, strained and reluctant. "Soon."

"Yes."

"Tomorrow night, at six? Dinner, a movie, anything you want."

Meghan made some kind of appropriate response, but the minute he was gone, she leaned against the door, needing its support. Several different emotions buzzed around her head. She felt disappointed that the kiss had been so short, and at the same time electrified and thrilled. With that brief kiss had come an immeasurable flash of excitement. She lifted her fingertips to her lips and examined them, half expecting there to be some lasting evidence of his touch. Her heart was pounding so hard, she felt as if her ribs were about to collapse. It wasn't that she'd never been kissed before; but no one had ever caused her pulse to react like this.

No one.

Chapter Four

The dishwasher was humming softly in the background when Meghan stepped into the shower late Saturday afternoon. She'd gone shopping and splurged on a new outfit, and had gotten home later than she would have liked. Normally she would have waited until the dishwasher was finished, but there wasn't time.

From the moment Grey had left her apartment the night before, her mind had been filled with romantic daydreams. She pictured him wining and dining her and then leading her onto a dance floor. Her fantasy showed him wrapping his arms around her and gazing into her eyes with undisguised admiration. Visions of him holding and kissing her filled her mind. Everything about this night was going to be perfect. They'd had such a rocky beginning, and she longed to make everything right between them.

Halfway through the shower, the water went freezing cold. Crying out in protest, Meghan turned off the knob and reached for a thick towel. A faint gurgling sound could be heard in the background. Thinking she should probably look into what was happening, Meghan wrapped the towel around her body and traipsed into the kitchen. Her wet hair fell over her face and she impatiently swatted it aside as she investigated the scene. An icy cold, wet sensation struck her toes the instant she moved onto the linoleum floor.

Meghan gasped and hurried back onto the carpet on her tiptoes.

Her dishwasher had overflowed.

"Oh, great," she moaned, running into the bathroom for some towels. As luck would have it, there was only one dry one and she was forced to search frantically through her laundry hamper for something to sop up the liquid. In her desperation she was tossing clothing left and right, hurling her panties and bras above her head.

Gathering up what she could, she hauled an armload of soiled clothes into the kitchen and quickly spread them over the floor. The first thing she had to do was to soak up as much water as she could as fast as possible. The whole time she was working, she was glancing at the clock.

What towels she could locate, plus a couple of shirts and two pairs of jeans, looked like mismatched puzzle pieces across her linoleum by the time she finished spreading them around. Still, water was puddled everywhere.

In an effort to help her clothes absorb as much as possible, Meghan danced over them, stomping her feet in a wild kind of jitterbug.

The doorbell chimed and Meghan froze. Please, she prayed, don't let that be Grey! Her gaze swung to the kitchen clock. It was still five minutes early. If there was a God in heaven, then it wouldn't be Grey at her front door.

"Who is it?" she called out, holding the front of her housecoat together with one hand, bunching the material together so tightly her nails threatened to bend. Her hair was half dry by this time and stuck out in several different directions.

"It's Grey."

Meghan's faith in the existence of a superior being descended by several notches. She couldn't answer the door dressed in her robe and underwear with her hair resembling something out of a science-fiction movie. If that wasn't bad enough, her kitchen floor looked as if several bodies had recently been vaporized.

"Meghan?"

"Ah . . . I'm not quite ready," she responded, forcing a cheerful note into her voice. "Would it be possible for you to come back in a few minutes?"

A throbbing silence followed her request.

"That is if it wouldn't be too much of an inconvenience," she tried again, desperately hoping he would agree. When he returned she'd explain, but she couldn't let him see her like this.

"I did say six, didn't I?" he pressed.

"Yes," Meghan muttered.

"Then it's all too obvious that something else, or more likely *someone else*, has come by," Grey called back to her. "How long would you like me to disappear for? An hour? Two? Will that be long enough for you?"

Someone else! Grey thought she was trying to get rid of him because there was a man in the apartment with her. Her shoulders sagged in defeat. Without hesitating any longer, she yanked open the front door and stepped aside.

"You might as well come in and have a good laugh," she said, sweeping her hand in front of her. To her horror, her voice became a high-pitched screech, barely discernible. She tried several times to swallow, but all she could manage was to make more of the same wretched sounds.

She dared not look at him, because once she saw the dismay in his eyes, she was bound to burst into tears, and that would only humiliate her further.

"Meghan, dear God, what happened?" He moved into her apartment and closed the door.

Her head hung so low that her chin was tucked against her collarbone. "I was in the shower when I heard funny gurgling noises.... My dishwasher died and there's water everywhere and I look like something from outer space." Desperate for oxygen, she sucked in a huge breath.

"Why didn't you say so in the first place?" Grey demanded.

He sounded almost angry, as though she'd purposely planned the whole disaster to evoke sympathy from him. "I wanted everything to be so special tonight—and you think I'm keeping a man in here." She didn't dare admit that he was the only male she'd thought about from the minute he'd stepped into Rose's Diner. Her shoulders jerked up and down each time she tried to breathe.

"Meghan," he said, appealing to her with his hands. "I don't know what to say. I'm sorry, I thought—"

"I know exactly what you thought," she interrupted as the situation and his initial reaction started to get the better of her. "As you can see, something *has* come up and I won't be able to go out tonight." Pointedly she walked over to the door and opened it for him.

"The least I can do is help," he insisted, apparently properly chagrined.

Somehow the picture of Professor Grey Carlyle under a sink refused to take shape in her mind. This was a man familiar with George Bernard Shaw—not water pipes and broken-down dishwashers.

"I doubt that you know the least bit about plumbing," she remarked stiffly.

"I don't," he agreed, and then added under his breath, "and even less about women, it seems."

With her chin tilted at a defiant angle, Meghan stood with her back straight, her fingers tightening around the doorknob. "I appreciate the offer, but no thanks."

"You're sure you'll be all right?"

"Positive," she said, and flipped a damp strand of hair out of her eyes with as much dignity as she could muster, which wasn't much.

He proceeded to walk out but paused just outside the apartment door to exhale sharply and murmured, "I'm sorry, Meghan."

"So am I," she responded, feeling both miserable and defeated.

Ten minutes later, after Meghan had dressed and run a brush through her hair, she phoned the apartment manager, who was gone for the evening—naturally. Given no other choice, Meghan phoned her father.

Perhaps she'd been a bit hasty with Grey, she mused in the quiet minutes that followed her call home. He'd only been trying to help. Unfortunately his offer had followed on the heels of his implication that she was hiding a man in her apartment. For him to even suggest such a thing was enough to set her teeth on edge.

Both Meghan's parents arrived within the half hour.

"Hi, Mom. Hi, Dad," she greeted, hugging them both, grateful for their love and support.

Her father carried a toolbox with him. At fifty, Patrick O'Day was in his prime—healthy, fit, and handsome to boot. Meghan had always been close to both parents.

"What happened in your kitchen? A mass murder?" her father teased, then laughed at his own joke as he stepped over the sopping array of clothes.

"Thanks for coming over," Meghan told him sincerely. "I don't know what I would have done. The apartment manager wasn't in and more than likely he wouldn't be able to get anyone here until Monday morning, anyway."

Colleen O'Day removed her coat while studying Meghan. "Weren't you going out with that professor friend of yours this evening?"

In her excitement Meghan had phoned her mother and told her all about meeting Grey. "*Was* as in past tense! Obviously, something came up."

"Meghan, darlin', you must be so disappointed."

She nodded. There didn't seem to be anything more to say. This evening wasn't turning out the least bit the way she'd hoped.

When it came to Grey, she felt like someone eager to appear in a circus performing in the high-wire balancing act. Although she wanted badly to do it, she couldn't seem to find her footing. Each time she tried, she nearly slipped and fell.

"You look tired," her mother said next.

Meghan felt exhausted. For most of the day she'd been running on nervous energy, not taking time to eat lunch. Breakfast had been a glass of orange juice and an English muffin while on the run.

"It's not your dishwasher—you've got a broken pipe down here," her father shouted from beneath the kitchen sink.

"Surprise, surprise," Meghan answered with a soft chuckle. With her mother's help she removed the clothes and towels that littered the floor, placing them inside the empty laundry basket.

Her father had nearly completed the repair when her doorbell chimed. The teakettle whistled at almost the same second, and frustrated, Meghan paused, not knowing which to attend to first.

"You get the door," her mother suggested, "and I'll take care of the tea."

It was Grey. He'd changed out of his pin-striped suit and into slacks and a sweater. He stood in front of her, holding a large book at his side.

"Before you get upset," he said, "I want you to know something."

Meghan's fingers curled around the doorknob. "You should know something, too," she returned.

"What?"

"I *have* got a man in my apartment—a handsome one who openly admits he loves me. This guy's crazy about me. Would you care to meet him?"

Anger flickered in Grey's eyes, and his mouth narrowed. A muscle at the side of his tightly clenched jaw quivered slightly.

"Meghan?" her mother called out from behind her. "Who is that at the door?"

Reluctantly Meghan stepped aside. "Mom and Dad, I'd like you both to meet Professor Grey Carlyle. He teaches English literature at Friends University."

Grey stepped into the apartment, but his heated gaze centered on Meghan. "Your father?" he whispered.

She gave him a saucy grin.

"Professor Carlyle, how pleased we are to meet you," Colleen O'Day greeted, looking absolutely delighted to make his acquaintance.

Her father rose awkwardly to his feet and held out his hand to Grey, who shook it. "It seems my daughter was stuck in some hot water," Pat joked, "and had to call on her old man to rescue her."

"We were just about to have some tea, Professor. Thankfully, Meghan's kettle was already filled with water. Won't you join us?"

Grey turned to Meghan, who didn't give him any indication she cared one way or the other. Actually, her heart was pounding so hard it was a wonder he couldn't see it beating against her sweatshirt.

"Thank you," he said, smiling up at Meghan's mother. "I'd enjoy a cup of tea."

"Pat?" Colleen asked, while Meghan brought cups down from the cupboard.

"Please." His reply was muffled as he was back under the sink.

"Can I do anything to help?" Grey asked, setting the book on the tabletop.

For the first time, Meghan could see the title, and when she did, she regretted her earlier display of anger. Grey had gone out and bought a book on plumbing repairs. Her insides went all soft at the thought that he should care so much.

"I'm almost finished here," her father told him. "I'll be with you in a couple of minutes. You sit down and I'll be there once I get this blasted fitting secure."

Her mother was busy pouring tea, which Meghan delivered to the small round table.

"I hope you're still hungry," Grey said when she approached him.

Her gaze shot to him and she blinked, not sure she understood.

"I've got two Chinese dinners in my car."

"I—"

"Why, that's thoughtful, isn't it, Meghan?" her mother interrupted. "Pat, don't you think we should be heading home right away? Danny needs to be picked up from the theater soon."

"I was going to have tea," he objected, then hesitated, apparently reading his wife's expression. "Right," he said evenly. "I forgot Danny. Now that your pipe's fixed, Meghan, I guess I'll be leaving." Her father picked up the pliers and the other things he'd been using and placed them inside his toolbox.

"Speaking of dinner," Colleen O'Day said, "why don't you come over to our house tomorrow for Sunday dinner, Professor? We've hardly had a chance to get to know you, and that way you could meet Meghan's three younger brothers."

Meghan's sip of tea moved halfway down her throat and refused to go any farther. It took several attempts to swallow it. Meghan didn't know what her mother could be thinking. Grey didn't want to meet her family. Why should he? He and Meghan barely knew each other, and every time they even tried to date, the evening ended in disaster.

"Thank you, Mrs. O'Day, I'd be honored."

Meghan realized his acceptance was only an excuse to be polite. After her parents left, she would let Grey know he shouldn't feel obligated.

"Okay, princess, everything seems to be working." To prove his point, Pat O'Day turned on the kitchen faucet, and after a few sputters the water gushed out normally.

"Thanks, Dad," she told him, kissing him on the cheek.

"It was a pleasure to have met you both," Grey said, in what Meghan was sure was his most courteous voice.

"You, too."

"We'll see you tomorrow at three, then," her mother prompted.

"I'll be there."

"Now, you two young folks try to enjoy the rest of your evening," Colleen O'Day suggested.

"We'll do that," Grey promised, his gaze reaching out and capturing Meghan's.

Chapter Five

Meghan braced her feet on the chair beside her, her knees raised as she held the small white box of spicy diced chicken directly below her chin. Grey might be accustomed to eating with chopsticks, but she wasn't.

"You're doing great."

She smiled lamely. "Right! I've got five different kinds of sauces smeared over the front of my sweatshirt and soy sauce dribbling down my chin." The piece of chicken that was balanced precariously on the end of her chopstick fell and landed in her lap, proving her point.

"Here." Grey handed her a paper napkin.

"Thanks."

Grey set aside the white container and reached for a small bag. "Are you ready for your fortune cookie?"

"Sure." She held out her hand, eager to discover her fate.

Grey gave her one and then promptly opened his first.

Meghan giggled at his shocked expression. "What does it say?"

"Ver-r-y inter-r-esting," he said in a feigned Chinese accent. "Cookie say professor must beware of waitress who read Shakespeare."

"Very funny," she returned, having a difficult time holding in her laughter. Setting aside the take-out container Meghan ceremonially split open her own fortune cookie.

"Well?" Grey prompted.

"It says I should beware of man who insists women eat with chopsticks."

Grey grinned. "I guess I asked for that."

"You most certainly did," she chided. "I don't suppose you want to hear my views on Shakespeare, do you?"

"Dear heavens, no. When it comes to literature, we can't seem to agree on anything."

"Literature," she echoed, "and just about everything else." That could very well be true, but when he was looking at her like this, his blue eyes warm and filled with humor, every argument she'd ever presented him with turned into melted ice cream. She was forced to pull her gaze away for fear of what he would read in her eyes.

"You'll be pleasantly surprised to know I'm crazy about Willie boy," she announced, popping half the fortune cookie into her mouth.

"Willie boy?"

"William Shakespeare."

"My faith in you has been restored," he said solemnly, dipping his head slightly.

"Oh, come now, Grey. Who couldn't like Shakespeare?"

"The same person who finds fault with Edmund Spenser is questioning my reserve toward another English great?" he asked, his eyes as round as paper plates. "I'd like to keep the peace as long as possible, if I can."

"Okay, okay. Forget I asked that." Still smiling, she stood and started to deposit the empty cartons into the garbage can.

Grey helped her. "Are you willing to discuss something else?" he asked.

He was so casual that Meghan assumed he was about to pitch another joke her way. "Now that all depends," she replied and tossed a wadded paper sack from behind her back. Her throw was a dead ringer, landing in the garbage can as though it were impossible for her to ever miss. Stunned, her mouth sagged open. "Did you see that?"

"Meghan, I'm serious."

She dropped her hands to her sides and turned to face him. "I know," she teased, laughter bubbling up inside her, "but I'm hoping once you get to know me, you'll lighten up a little."

His responding smile was feeble at best. "Meghan, would you please listen to me?"

The smile drained from her eyes when she realized that something was indeed bothering him. "Yes, of course."

He buried his hands in his pockets and walked over to the sink, staring at it for a couple of seconds before turning to face her. "Earlier, when I met your parents..."

"Yes?"

"I saw your face when your mother invited me to Sunday dinner. You weren't pleased. The fact is, you don't want me there, do you?"

Her first thought was to confirm his suspicion, but she realized it wasn't entirely true. She *did* long for him to meet her family, only she feared the outcome. "You're more than welcome," she said blithely, hoping to casually dismiss any reserve he'd sensed. "It's just that . . ."

"What?"

"I don't want you to feel obligated. Mom's one of those warm, wonderful people who insists on sweeping everyone she meets under her wing. I'm afraid you might feel pressured into joining my family just because my mother issued the invitation. If the plumber had been here, she probably would have invited him, too," Meghan said, making light of her parent's offer. "It's just Mom's way."

"I see."

From the stiff tone of his voice, it was clear Grey obviously didn't. "You have to understand," Meghan hurried to add. "My brothers would love nothing better than to get you involved in a hot little contest of touch football. And knowing Dad, he'd corner you the minute you walk in the door. He loves chess—anyone visiting is fair game. My dad's a wonderful man but he tends to be something of a poor loser." Meghan realized she was rambling, but she was frantically trying to make him believe that she had his best interests at heart. She didn't even mention the ribbing her three brothers would likely give him. The annoyed look Grey was giving her told her she was apparently doing a poor job of explaining the situation.

"But what it really boils down to is that I wouldn't fit in with your family," he announced starkly. "That's what you're really trying to say."

"Not entirely." It was; only she hadn't fully realized it. "You're welcome to come if that's what you want," she finished, feeling both frustrated and confused.

"You mean your mother's welcome is sincere, but yours isn't?"

"Oh, Grey, why do you have to complicate this? I told you the reasons I have my doubts, but whether you decide to come or not is entirely up to you."

"I see."

Meghan slapped her hands noisily against the sides of her legs. "I wish you would stop saying that."

"What?"

"*I see*, in that pitiful voice, as though I'd casually insulted you." Earlier they'd sat and joked and teased each other like longtime friends, and now they were snapping at one another like cantankerous turtles. In the short time since they'd met, they'd muddled their way through several disputes. The last thing Meghan wanted was another one.

"I see," Gray said in exactly the tone she'd been talking about.

Meghan burst out laughing. She couldn't help herself, although it was clear that this reaction was the last thing Grey had expected of her.

"Professor Grey Carlyle, come here."

"Why?" His brows arched suspiciously, he studied her, clearly not trusting her.

"Never mind, I'll come to you." She did so, but the few short steps that separated them seemed more like miles. By the time she stood directly in front of him,

Meghan had nearly lost her nerve. Boldly she slipped her arms around his neck, tilted back her head and gazed squarely into his eyes.

Grey held himself stiff, with his hands hanging loosely at this sides, his brow puckered. "Kindly explain what you're doing!"

"You mean to tell me you don't know?" she asked softly. His mouth was scant inches from her own. Their soft, short breaths mingled and merged.

Very slowly, Meghan raised her lips to his and graced him with the briefest of kisses.

In response, Grey cleared his throat and moved his head farther away from hers, yet he didn't disentangle her arms from his neck or make any move to slip her out of his arms.

If he expected to thwart her with a scowl, it wouldn't work. Meghan stood on the tips of her toes and leisurely passed her mouth over his in a soft, almost chaste kiss.

This time neither moved, neither breathed. Kissing Grey the first time should have been warning enough. The second brief sampling only whetted Meghan's appetite for more.

His too, it seemed.

Grey lowered his head until his lips barely touched hers. He held himself completely immobile for a long moment, brushing his mouth back and forth over hers, savoring the velvet texture of her moist lips. The tip of his tongue outlined first her upper lip and then her bottom one until she felt her knees would buckle if he didn't give her a more complete taste. She moaned softly and he slipped his mouth over hers with a fierce kind of tenderness, molding her lips to his own.

His fingers were planted on the curves of her shoulders when he gently pushed her away. His breathing was deep and ragged. Meghan's own wasn't any more controlled.

She'd meant to entice him, to take his mind off her mother's invitation to Sunday dinner and the problem that had created between them. Instead, Meghan's plan had backfired.

Everything went stock still. She swallowed uncomfortably and lowered her eyes. She couldn't have met his look, had the defense of Mother Earth depended upon it.

"Meghan?"

"I . . . I shouldn't have done that."

"Yes," he murmured, "you should have." He lifted his hand to her nape, urging her back into his arms. Without any argument, she went. This diversion she'd initiated wasn't a game any longer. She was trembling, with both excitement and need.

Grey kissed her again, using his tongue to coax her lips farther apart. When she responded, his tongue slid gently into her mouth, sending a wild jolt of elation through her body.

By the time Grey's lips moved from hers and he buried his face in the curve of her neck, Meghan had no strength left in her bones.

"All right," he whispered into her hair. "I'll conveniently forget the dinner tomorrow. You needn't worry I'll show up—I'll find some excuse to give your mother later."

Meghan tightened her arms around his neck. "I want you there. Only please remember what I said."

He laughed softly. "Meghan, it was obvious from the first that you didn't."

"I changed my mind," she said more forcefully this time. "Just be prepared for . . . my family."

"I suppose you're going to suggest I throw a game of chess, as well."

"That would be nice, but not necessary. It's time Dad owned up to the fact his strategy stinks."

A long moment passed in which Meghan felt they did nothing more than enjoy the feel of each other.

When her legs felt as if they could support her, she stepped away from him, but her heart was pounding like a charging locomotive. And yet she felt as weak as a newborn kitten.

"Please come," she said in as firm a voice as she could manage.

"You're sure?"

She pressed her forehead against his chest. "Yes."

"Then I'll be there."

Meghan was in the kitchen with her mother, peeling a huge pile of potatoes, when the doorbell chimed in the background. Ripping the apron from the front of her dress, she heaved in a calming breath to regain her composure and hurried into the living room.

Her parents' home was an older style built in the late 1920s, with a huge drawing room. An old brick fireplace with mantel was situated at one end, and bookcases along the other. A sofa, a recliner and two matching chairs with ottomans filled the rectangular area and were positioned around the television, where her father and brothers were watching a football game.

"That's probably Grey," she announced dramatically, standing in front of the TV set. It was the only way to completely gain their attention. "Now, please remember what I said," she cautioned, eyeing them severely.

"Oh, Meghan," thirteen-year-old Danny cried. "You make it sound like we're going to hurt him. He mustn't be much of a man if he can't hold his own in a little game of touch football."

"We've already been through this once, Daniel O'Day. You're not going to ask him to play football with you. Understand?"

"You sweet on this guy, Sis?" Brian asked, eyeing her with sparkling blue eyes and a mischievous grin.

"That's none of your business." As a high-school senior, Brian should know better than to ask. Meghan expected a little more understanding from her oldest brother. It was obvious, however, that she wasn't going to get it. Her mistake had been revealing to her younger siblings how much she *did* care about Grey.

"Dad . . . No chess, please."

"Princess, are you going to open the door or not? You're leaving the poor man to freeze to death on the front porch while you give everyone instructions on how to act around him."

"Grey's important to me."

"Oh, gee," fifteen-year-old Chad said, and hit his forehead with the palm of his hand. "We hadn't figured that one out, Sis."

Meghan stood in front of the door, sighed inwardly and smoothed her hands down the front of her dress. At the last moment, she twirled around and faced her father and brothers once more. "Please."

"Meghan, for heaven's sake just answer the door."

She did as her father requested, her smile forced. "Hello, Grey," she said greeting him with a wide smile and opening the screen door for him. "I'm pleased you could make it."

Grey stepped into the family home, carrying a bouquet of red rosebuds. He was dressed in a suit and tie, looking as dignified and professional as ever.

Meghan looped her arm around his elbow so they faced the O'Day men as a united force. "You remember my dad from last night?"

"Of course." Grey stepped forward and the two men shook hands.

Brian stood with his father and Meghan introduced him.

"I'm pleased to meet you, Brian."

"You too, Professor."

"Please call me Grey."

"Can I call you that, too?" Chad asked. He wasn't wearing his shoes, and his socks had huge holes in the toes.

"That's Chad," Meghan said, and prayed Grey didn't notice her brother's feet.

"I'm fifteen. How old are you?"

"Chad!" Meghan cried, closing her eyes.

"He looks too old for you, Meghan," Chad muttered under his breath. "Now I suppose you're going to get all mad at me because I said so."

She offered Grey a weak smile, which was the best she could do.

"I'm thirty-four," Grey answered without a pause. "And you're right, I *am* too old for Meghan."

"No, you're not," Danny piped up, walking over and holding out his hand, which Grey readily accepted. "I'm Danny."

Meghan could have kissed the freckles off her youngest brother's nose at that moment. Grey wasn't too old for her. In fact, their age difference had never come up before as she hadn't given the matter a second thought.

Danny, however, quickly destroyed all her goodwill by adding, "So, you don't play football? I always hoped that when Meghan got married her husband would like sports."

"Danny!" Meghan cried, feeling her face explode with color. "Professor Carlyle and I are just getting to know each other. We aren't going to be married."

"You're not?"

"Of course not. We only met a few days ago."

"Yeah, but from the way you've been acting all afternoon, I thought you were really hot for this guy."

Meghan cast him a look heated enough to boil water.

"All right, all right," Danny moaned. "I'll shut up."

"Meghan," her father advised discreetly, "if you let go of Grey's arm, he might be able to take off his coat and sit down."

"Oh, sorry," she said, smiling apologetically. She cast Grey a knowing glance and whispered, "I warned you."

"So you did," he mumbled back and removed his overcoat, keeping the bouquet of flowers with him.

"Would you like some tea or coffee or anything else?" Meghan asked him, just as her mother stepped into the room.

"Professor, how good of you to come," Colleen said graciously.

Grey handed her the roses. "Thank you for asking me, Mrs. O'Day."

"Colleen, please," she corrected. "Oh, my! Roses! Really, Professor, you shouldn't have, but I'm glad you did. It's been years since I've received anything so lovely."

"You brought the roses for my mom?" Danny asked incredulously. "What did you bring for Meghan? I thought you were sweet on *her*. You better watch it, 'cause she's got a temper."

"Danny," Meghan whispered, her eyes pleading with his. "Please don't say another word. Not one more word!"

"But . . ."

"Do me a favor and keep quiet for the rest of the afternoon."

The injustice of it all was nearly more than her youngest sibling could take and he tucked his arms over his chest and centered his concentration on the football game that blared from the television set.

"How are the Chiefs doing?" Grey asked, sitting down in the chair beside her father.

"Terrible," Pat O'Day muttered and sadly shook his head. "The Seahawks are running all over them. What they need is more power in the backfield."

"Dad's something of an armchair quarterback," Meghan explained.

"Do you like football, Professor?" Chad asked, leaning forward from his position on the ottoman, his hands clasped. His gaze was intent, as though the outcome of Grey's relationship with the O'Day family rested on his reply.

"I've been known to watch a game every now and again," Grey answered.

Meghan sighed her relief.

"That's great, because us men usually play a game or two ourselves after dinner," Chad informed him, as though expecting Grey to volunteer to join them.

It was all Meghan could do to keep from jumping up and down and waving her arms in an effort to remind her brothers of their talk. They'd promised not to involve Grey in any of this, but it looked as if Chad had conveniently forgotten.

"I'll take the flowers into the kitchen. Thank you again, Professor," Colleen said, gently sniffing them and smiling proudly. She turned toward her husband and sons. "Dinner will be ready in thirty minutes, so don't get so involved in this silly football game."

"Don't worry, Mom," Brian said. "The Chiefs are losing."

Meghan stood, her feet braced apart. She would have remained planted there, had her mother not dragged her back into the kitchen.

"Mom," she protested, looking back at Grey. "It's not safe in there for him. Grey isn't like other men."

"Oh?" Her mother's eyebrows arched speculatively and her eyes twinkled with amusement.

What Meghan really meant to say was that Grey wasn't anything like the other men she'd dated over the past few years. He was special, and she didn't want anything to happen that would destroy their budding relationship.

"I mean—" she hurried to add "—Grey's an only child. His whole life has revolved around academia. All Brian, Chad and Danny know is football. Grey was so smart he was sent to an advanced preschool class, for heaven's sake." Her mother looked impressed and Meghan continued, listing the details of his academic achievements. "From kindergarten he went straight into a gifted-students program. Grey's a lamb among wolves in there with Dad and the boys.''

''He'll do just fine,'' her mother returned confidently.

''But—''

''Now come on, fretting isn't going to do any good, and neither is hurrying in there to rescue him from the fiendish plots of your younger brothers.''

Meghan cast a longing glance over her shoulder, knowing her mother was right but still having problems not running interference. Grey meant more to her than any man she'd ever met. She and Grey were vastly different—almost complete opposites—and yet they shared several common interests. Meghan's biggest fear, now that she'd had time to analyze it, was that his meeting her family would emphasize how different they were and discourage Grey from continuing their promising relationship.

''I'll set the table,'' Meghan offered when she'd finished dicing the tomato for the salad. The dining room was situated between the living room and the kitchen and offered Meghan the opportunity to check on Grey without being obvious. She opened the drawer to the china hutch and brought out the lace tablecloth. While she was there, she stuck her head around the corner and chanced a peek inside the living room. To her dismay, she discovered Grey and her father deeply involved in a game of chess. She groaned and pressed her forehead against the wall. As much as she loved her father, when it came to chess he was a fanatic and even worse, a terrible sport.

By the time Meghan finished setting the table and mashing the potatoes, dinner was ready. She stood with her hands braced against the back of a dining-room chair while the men gathered around the table.

"Professor, please sit next to Meghan," Colleen O'Day instructed, pointing toward the empty chair beside her daughter.

Grey moved to her side.

"I saw you and Dad," she muttered out of the side of her mouth. "How'd it go?"

"He won."

Meghan sighed, appeased. "Thank you," she whispered back.

"Fair and square, Meghan. I didn't throw the game."

"Dad won?" she asked, louder this time, her voice filled with surprise. She blinked a couple of times, hardly able to believe what she was hearing.

"I'm the world's worst chess player, only you never bothered to ask."

A smile quivered at the corners of her mouth and she shook her head. Once her father had claimed his place at the head of the table, the family bowed their heads as Pat O'Day offered the blessing.

Meals had always been a happy, sharing time for the O'Days, and Danny started in talking about what was lacking on the Kansas City Chiefs football team.

The buttermilk biscuits were passed around, followed by Yankee pot roast, mashed potatoes, thick gravy, small green peas and the fresh salad.

"Professor, Meghan was telling me you graduated from high school when you were fourteen," her mother stated conversationally, turning the subject away from football.

"Is that true?" Chad popped half a biscuit into his mouth and stared at Grey as if the older man had recently stepped off a spaceship.

Grey cleared his throat and looked self-conscious. "Yes."

Colleen O'Day looked on proudly. "Meghan was always the one who earned top marks in our family."

"That's because she's a girl," Danny objected. "Girls always do better in school—teachers like them better. Only sissies get good grades." As if he suddenly realized what he'd said, Danny's gaze shot to Grey and he quickly lowered his eyes. "Not *all* boys who get good grades are nerds, though."

Meghan wanted to kick Danny under the table, but she dared not. She was pleased that her mother didn't continue to drill Grey about his education. She could well imagine what her brothers would say if they knew he'd zipped through college and gone directly into a doctoral program. From there, he'd been accepted on the faculty of Friends University where he'd taught ever since.

"What about girls?" Brian asked, directing the question to Grey. "I mean, if you were so much younger than everyone else, who was there for you to date?"

"No one," Grey admitted frankly. "I didn't know many girls, as it was. There weren't any my age in the neighborhood and none at school, either. Until I was in my twenties, I rarely had anything to do with the opposite sex."

"Personally, I don't think they're worth the trouble," Danny said, completely serious. "Brian used to think that way, but then he met Peggy and he's gone to the other side. Chad's not much better. There's a girl who calls him all the time and he takes the phone into the hall closet and talks for hours at a time. I think he's turning traitor, too.''

"It happens that way sometimes," Grey commented, sharing a knowing look with Meghan and doing an admirable job of disguising his amusement.

"You like my sister, don't you?" Danny continued, then added before Grey could answer, "I guess that's all right if she likes you. And she does. You wouldn't believe it. From the moment she arrived this morning, all she's done is give us instructions on what we could say to you and what we couldn't. I've forgotten half the stuff already.''

"Obviously," Meghan said wryly.

"I think I can understand why Meghan likes you so much," Chad said with a thoughtful stare. "You teach literature, and Meghan really loves that stuff. She's always reading books dead people wrote.''

Meghan stood abruptly and braced her hands against the edge of the table. "Anyone for dessert?''

An hour later, Meghan was helping her mother with the last of the dishes. Brian had cleared the table and the other boys had dealt with the leftovers and loading the dishwasher, leaving the few pots and pans that needed to be washed by hand. Grey and her father were in the living room playing a second game of chess.

"Meghan," her mother said with an expressive sigh, "I wish you'd relax. Grey is doing just fine.''

"I know," she said, rubbing the palms of her hands together. "I suppose I'm overreacting, but I wanted him to feel at home with all of us, and I don't know if that's possible with the boys.''

"He seems to be taking their teasing in his stride."

"What else can he do?" she exclaimed. "Challenge Danny to a duel?"

Her mother laughed at that. "I told you before, there was nothing to worry about." She wiped her hands dry and reached for the hand lotion. "You like Grey, don't you, princess? More than anyone in a long while."

"Oh, Mom, I couldn't have made that any more obvious."

Colleen O'Day chuckled. "You're right about that."

"But we're so different." She tucked an errant reddish curl around her ear and cast her gaze to the floor. She was Yankee pot roast and Grey was T-bone steak. "I like him so much, but he's so intelligent...."

"So are you," her mother countered.

"Educated."

"You're self-taught. You may not have an extensive education, but you've always had an inquiring mind and a hunger for the written word. Grey wouldn't be attracted to you if you weren't bright."

"But he's so dignified and proud."

Her mother continued spreading the cream over her hands, composing her thoughts. "I don't see any real problem there. Just don't wear your purple tennis shoes around him."

Meghan laughed, then chewed on the corner of her mouth. "I'm crazy about him, Mom, but I'm afraid I'm closing my eyes to reality. I can't understand why Grey is interested in me. It won't last, and I'm so afraid of falling in love with him. I expect him to open his eyes any minute and realize how irrational our being together is. It would devastate me. I'm excited and afraid at the same time.''

Her mother was silent for a long moment. ''When you were four years old, you were reading.''

''What has that got to do with anything?''

Her mother smiled faintly. ''From the time you could walk you were hauling books around with you everywhere you went. You were bound and determined to find out what all those letters meant and all their sounds. I don't suppose you remember the way you used to follow me through the house, pestering the life out of me until I'd give up and sit down with you. Once you were able to connect the letters with the sounds, you were on your own and there was no holding you back.''

''It's not letters and sounds that I'm dealing with now. It's a man, and I feel so unsure of myself.''

''Let your heart guide you, princess. You've always been sensible when it comes to relationships. You're not one to fall head over heels in love at the drop of a hat. If you feel so strongly about Grey, even if you've only known him a short time, then all I can advise you is to trust yourself.''

''There isn't anything else I can do, is there?''

''He's a good man.''

''I know.''

Meghan's father drifted into the kitchen and reached for a leftover buttermilk biscuit. He paused and chuckled. ''I've got to hand it to that young man of yours,'' he said to Meghan.

''What, Dad?'' Meghan fully expected him to comment on the chess game.

''Chad and Danny talked him into playing football. They're in the front yard now.''

Chapter Six

"But Grey's wearing a suit!" Meghan burst out as though that fact alone would prevent him from participating in any form of physical activity.

"Brian lent him an old sweatshirt of his."

"Oh, dear Lord," Meghan cried, rushing toward the front of the house.

"He doesn't need you," her father called after her. "Your professor friend is perfectly capable of taking care of himself, don't you think?"

"Against Chad and Danny?" she challenged. "And Brian?"

Her father responded with a tight frown. "On second thought, maybe you'd better check on him."

Meghan grabbed her coat from the hall closet on her way out the door. Her first thought was to dash onto the lawn and insist all four of them stop their foolishness this minute. Instead, she stood on the porch with her hand over her mouth as she watched the unfolding scene.

Grey was bent forward, his hands braced against his knees. After shouting out a long series of meaningless numbers, Brian took several steps in reverse and lobbed the football to Grey. The ball soared through the air, the entire length of the yard, and no one looked more shocked than Chad and Danny when Grey caught it.

"Go for the touchdown!" Brian screamed at the top of his lungs.

"No!" Meghan called out. Unable to watch, she covered her face with both hands. A chill rippled down her spine that had nothing to do with the frosty November weather. Part of her longed to charge into the middle of their scrimmage and yank Grey off the grass before he got hurt, but she had no right to act as his guardian. As an adult, he must have known what he was getting himself into when he agreed to this craziness. He would be lucky, though, if he came out of this with nothing more than a broken bone.

From the hoots and cheers that followed, it became apparent that Grey had either scored or that Chad and Danny had stopped him cold. She couldn't decide which, and dared not look.

"Meghan?"

She whirled around to find Grey standing on the top step of the porch, looking worried. Her breath left her lungs in a sudden rush of relief. "Are you all right?"

"I'm more concerned about you. You're as pale as a ghost."

"I thought Chad was going to tackle you."

"He had to catch me first. I may not know much about football, but I'm one hell of a sprinter."

Meghan's relief was so great that she impulsively tossed her arms around his neck and squeezed for all she was worth. He felt warm and solid against her and she buried her face in his neck, laughing and fighting off the urge to cry at the same time.

Chuckling, Grey wrapped his arms around her waist and swung her around. "I made a touchdown, and according to Brian, that makes me some kind of hero."

"Some kind of fool, you mean."

"You're not going to kiss her, are you?" Danny asked, making it sound the equivalent of picking up a slug.

Grey's gaze delved into Meghan's. He wanted to kiss her, she could tell, but he wouldn't. Not now. Later, his look promised. She answered him with a soft smile that claimed she was holding him to his word, even if it was unspoken.

"I think we better quit while we're ahead," Brian suggested, joining Meghan and Grey. "It's getting too dark, and personally, I don't think Meghan's heart can take much more of this. I thought she was going to faint when you caught that last pass."

"I was afraid Chad and Danny were going to murder him simply because he happened to catch it."

"We wouldn't have done that," Chad said with more than a hint of indignation. "This is touch football, remember?"

Danny scrunched up his face. "I might have tackled him, but I knew Meghan would kill me dead if I did."

Meghan looped her arm around Danny's neck in a headlock and rubbed her knuckles over the top of his head. "You're darn tootin', I would have."

With his arms squirming, her brother escaped and angrily glared at his older sister. "I hate it when you do that!"

Laughing, they all entered the house.

An hour later Grey followed Meghan back to her apartment and parked outside her building.

"Do you want to come up for coffee?" she asked. Looking at Grey now, she found it difficult to remember that he'd been playing football with her brothers only a short time earlier. His eyes were serious, his expression sober. He seemed reserved and quiet after an afternoon filled with noise and fun.

"I'd love to come up for coffee," he answered automatically and smiled at her softly, "but regrettably, I can't. There's enough paperwork stacked on my desk to keep me up most of the night." He reached out and caressed the side of her face with his finger. "I enjoyed today more than I can tell you, Meghan. You have a wonderful family."

"I think so." She was close to her parents and all her brothers, although she'd wanted to throttle the boys when she saw that they'd managed to drag Grey into a football game. What had surprised her most was Grey's unbridled willingness to partake in her brothers' folly.

He continued to gently stroke the side of her face. Meghan knew he planned to kiss her, and she met him halfway, automatically slipping her arms around his neck. He lowered his lips to caress hers in a long, tender, undemanding kiss. Meghan felt certain that he meant to kiss her once and then leave, but instead, he tightened his arms around her waist, bringing her closer to him. The kiss deepened and she was treated to a series of slow, compelling kisses that made her weak with longing. Something special had sprung into existence between them from the first moment they'd met—something delicate and so tangible that Meghan could feel it all the way to the marrow of her bones.

She moaned at the crescendoing ferocity of sensation that encircled her heart and her head. Grey responded immediately to her small sigh of pleasure by prolonging the kiss. He parted her lips, then teased and tormented her with his tongue until Meghan was dazed almost senseless.

"Oh, Meghan," he whispered into her hair as though in a state of shock himself. "I can't believe the things you do to me."

"Me?" she asked, her laugh soft and mildly hysterical. Surely he must know that whatever physical electricity existed between them was mutual.

Grey moved away from her and rested his head against the wall, taking in several giant gulps of air. "One kiss. I told myself I was only going to kiss you once. You're quickly becoming addictive, Meghan O'Day."

Meghan's breathing was ragged, as well. "I'm sorry you can't come in for coffee, but I understand," she told him when it was possible to do so and sound as if she had her wits about her. "I enjoyed today, too. Very much."

His hand reached for hers. "There's a cocktail party I have to attend next Saturday night. It'll be dry and boring and filled with people who will remind you of Fulton Essary." He paused and grinned wryly, before adding, "They'll remind you a lot of me, too. Will you go with me?"

Meghan's heart leaped to her throat. Grey had boldly walked into her world and was issuing an invitation for her to explore his. Doubts buzzed around her head like pesky mosquitos at a Fourth of July picnic. "Are you sure you want me there?"

"I've never been more confident of anything in my life. You'll do just fine."

Meghan wished she shared his faith in her. "Before you go, I want to tell you about a decision I recently made," she said, smiling up at him. This small piece of news was something she'd been saving all day to tell him. "I've decided to visit Friends tomorrow."

His gaze widened briefly. "'Visit'?"

"You told me one of the reasons you invited me to hear Dr. Essary was to expose me to the richness of education that was available at the university. I've concluded that you're right. My being older than most first-year students shouldn't matter. There's no time like the present to go back to school. I'm so excited, Grey. I feel like a little kid again, and I have you to thank for giving me the courage to do something I should have done long ago."

The warmth of his smile caused her heart to leap.

"Classes don't start until after Christmas, and I'm only going to sign up for two the first time around and see how I do. That way, I can keep working for a while, as well." She felt a spontaneous smile light up her face as the enthusiasm surged through her. "I'm really trying to be sensible about all this."

"I think that's wise."

"When I first leafed through the catalog, I wanted to register for every literature class offered. But the more I thought about it, the more I realized that I've got to ease my way back into the habit of going to school. After all, it's been several years since I graduated."

THE WAY TO A MAN'S HEART   83

"Meghan?"

He stopped her, and when she raised her gaze to his, she noted his brow had puckered into a frown. "Did you decide to take any of the classes I'll be teaching?"

She nodded eagerly. "The one on the American novel. But when I saw that we'd be reading *Moby Dick*, I had second and third thoughts."

"You don't like Melville?"

Meghan nearly laughed aloud at the look of dismay that briefly sparked in his clear blue eyes. "I read the book in high school and found it insufferable. All those allegories! And from what I see, they made such little sense."

Grey's frown darkened.

"He was a great writer, though," she said, hoping to appease Grey before she slipped into a black hole and couldn't find her way out. When it came to literature Meghan often found her views varied greatly from his. For the past two days, they'd been getting along so well that she'd forgotten how vehemently Grey defended the literary greats.

"Were you aware that *Moby Dick* is said to be the quintessential American novel?"

"I imagine Margaret Mitchell was upset when she heard that," Meghan returned jokingly. "Mark Twain, on the other hand, probably took the news in his stride."

"You can't compare those two to Melville."

What had started out in jest was quickly turning into something far more serious. "Grey, honestly, Melville was tedious and boring to the extreme. Maybe he would have appeared less so if he'd made even a passing effort to be less obtuse."

He looked away from her and expelled his breath. "I can't believe you actually said that."

"I can't, either," she confessed. Her quicksilver tongue wasn't helping matters any. She didn't want to argue with Grey. She wanted him to be as excited as she was about attending Friends. "I didn't mean to start a fight with you, Grey. I just wanted to thank you for encouraging me."

He nodded. Although Meghan assumed their disagreement had been a minor one quickly forgotten, Grey was silent on the short walk upstairs to her apartment. Brooding and thoughtful, as well, she noted.

"Thank you for bringing me home," she said.

"Meghan, listen." He paused and raked his fingers through his hair, looking uneasy. "I'd prefer it if you didn't sign up for any of my classes. It would be the best thing all the way around, don't you think?"

Those words felt like a bucket of cold water unexpectedly dumped over her head. She couldn't really blame Grey. Already she'd proved how opinionated and headstrong she was. He was looking for a way to avoid problems, and she couldn't blame him. If she were his student, she would be nothing but a damn nuisance. Her pride felt more than a little dented, but she could do nothing but bow to his wishes.

"Of course. If that's what you want," she agreed stiffly.

"It is."

She cast her gaze downward, feeling wretched and sorry now that she'd even told him her plans.

"Good night," he said, leaning forward enough to brush his mouth over her cheek.

"Good night," she replied, doing her best to force some enthusiasm into her voice.

He waited until she was inside the apartment and the living area was lighted before he left her. "I'll call you later in the week," he promised.

She nodded, forcing a smile. The minute she closed the door after him, the smile vanished. Dropping her purse on the recliner, she walked directly into the kitchen and braced her hands against the countertop and stared sightlessly at her microwave. The lump in her throat felt huge, and for a moment it was impossible to breathe.

Grey was well within his rights to ask her not to register for any of his classes, but she couldn't help taking it personally. She felt hurt and insulted.

An hour later, Meghan didn't feel much better. She sat in front of the television, wearing her yellow robe from Texas and watching a murder-mystery rerun. The phone rang, and heaving a sigh, she reached for it.

"Yo," she answered, certain it was her brother.

"Yo?" Grey returned, chuckling.

Meghan uncurled her bare feet from beneath her and straightened. "Grey?"

"Hello. I took a break a minute ago to make myself a cup of coffee and I got to thinking about something. When I asked you not to register for any of my classes, there was a very good reason."

Meghan already knew what that was, but she didn't volunteer the information.

"The thing is, Meghan, I want to continue being with you as much as I can. If you're taking my American-novel class, then it might border on the unethical for me to date you."

"Oh, Grey," she whispered, closing her eyes as a current of warm sensations washed over her. "I'm so glad you called. I was really feeling awful about it."

"Why didn't you say something?" he chided gently.

She brushed her bangs from her forehead and held her palm there. "I couldn't. I thought you objected because I can be so dogmatic and bullheaded when it comes to literature."

"I hadn't noticed," he teased.

"Oh, stop." But there was no censure in her voice. She felt as if a heavy weight had been lifted from her heart.

"You agree with me about not registering for my classes, don't you?"

"Of course. I should have realized why myself." She hadn't; and that only went to prove how insecure she felt about her relationship with him.

"Yes, you should have. I'm glad I phoned. I don't want any more discord between us. I guess for some people, politics is a touchy subject—for us it's literature."

Meghan chuckled. "You're right about that."

To enter the administration office at Friends University was like walking into a living nightmare. Bodies crammed each available space, and lines shot out in every direction imaginable. The noise was horrendous.

Once Meghan had managed to get inside the door, she heaved in a deep breath and started asking questions of the first person she could.

"Pardon me, can I register for classes in this line?" she asked a gum-chewing brunette.

"Not here, honey, this one's for those of us needing financial assistance. Try over there," the girl told her, pointing across the room.

Meghan groaned inwardly and was forced to traipse through a human obstacle course, stepping over and around bodies that took up nearly every inch of floor space, until she reached the far side of the building.

She found a line and stood there, praying she was in the right place.

"Hi," a deep male voice greeted from behind her. "You work at Rose's Diner, don't you?"

Meghan turned to face a tall, rakishly good-looking man who looked vaguely familiar. "Yes. Do I know you?"

"There's no reason you should. I eat at Rose's every now and again. I don't know if you've waited on me or not, but I remember you from there. My name is Eric Vogel."

"Hello, Eric. I'm Meghan O'Day," she replied above the noise and they exchanged handshakes. "This place is a madhouse, isn't it?"

"It's like this every quarter."

"Don't tell me that, please."

"You're a senior?"

"I wish," she said. "I haven't been to school in years, and I'm beginning to feel like an alien—in with all these eighteen- and twenty-year-olds."

"How old are you?"

"Twenty-four."

"Hey, me too."

"I guess that qualifies us for a senior-citizen discount," Meghan teased. "I sincerely hope I'm in the right line for registration."

"You are," Eric said confidently, easing the pack off his back and setting it on the floor.

He apparently knew far more than Meghan did, and she was grateful he'd struck up a conversation with her.

"What classes are you planning to take?"

Awkwardly Meghan opened the catalog and showed him the two literature classes she'd chosen earlier, after much internal debate. Eric instantly started questioning her about her choices and it soon became apparent that they shared a love for the classics.

"You'll like Dr. Murphy's class," Eric assured her. "It's a whirlwind tour through six hundred years of British rhyme."

"A poetry-in-motion sort of class, then."

"Right," Eric said with a low chuckle.

The urge to ask her newfound friend if he'd ever taken anything from Grey was almost overwhelming, but Meghan resisted.

"Once we're done here, do you want to go over to The Hub and have a cup of coffee?" Eric suggested. "I'm meeting my fiancée there, and a couple of other friends. Why don't you join us?"

"I'll be glad to," Meghan said eagerly. The line was moving at a snail's pace and by the time they'd finished, it could well be close to noon. The student center seemed as good a place as any to have lunch.

Eric must have been thinking the same thing. "We might as well plan on having lunch together, from the way things are going here."

"It certainly looks that way," Meghan agreed.

Eric continued to leaf through the catalog. "By the way, if you're interested in joining a reading group, there's one that meets Friday afternoons at two. We get together at The Hub, although I've got to confess we don't do as much reading as we'd like. Mostly we drink coffee and seek solutions to world problems. It's a literary group with bipartisan overtones, if you know what I mean. We seldom agree on anything, but love the challenge of a good argument.''

The group sounded like something Meghan had been looking to find for years. ''I'd love to come,'' she told him, having trouble keeping the excitement out of her voice.

Meghan had made her first college friend, and it felt good.

Grey's office lacked welcome when he let himself inside on Friday afternoon. He needed to phone Meghan and had put it off all week. He sat in his high-back leather chair and held a hand over his face as if the gesture would wipe out the image that kept popping into his mind.

He'd known Meghan was registering for classes Wednesday morning and had half expected her to stop off and see him afterward. When he'd talked to her the day before, he'd casually issued the invitation for her to come to his office, but he had a class at one and she had to be at Rose's before three, so the timing was iffy.

It had been pure chance that had taken Grey to The Hub early Wednesday afternoon. The faculty dining room was situated on the second floor and he was joining Dr. Riverside when he happened to catch sight of an auburn-haired woman who instantly reminded him of Meghan.

It *had* been Meghan, and a surge of adrenaline shot through him to have bumped into her so unexpectedly this way. It took a second longer for Grey to notice the two men and another woman who were sitting at the table with her. The four were talking and laughing, obviously enjoying getting to know one another. One of the men, clearly attracted to her and doing his best to make himself noticed, had his arm draped along the back of her chair. He looked like a decent sort—clean-cut, preppy. Although it was difficult to tell from this distance, Grey thought he might have had the fellow in one of his classes a couple of years before. The arm looped over Meghan's chair was in no way territorial, but the emotions that shot through Grey certainly were. He felt downright jealous, and the fact stunned him. He had no right to feel so strongly about Meghan. Knowing he could experience such a powerful emotion toward her after so short an acquaintance shook him to the core. He'd left as soon as he could make his excuses to Dr. Riverside and returned to his office, badly shaken by the incident.

Two days had passed and Grey had yet to erase the image of Meghan from his mind. She hadn't stopped off at his office that afternoon, which had been just as well; she belonged with her friends. As soon as her classes started up, after the first of the year, she would come into contact with others like the ones she'd met Wednesday. With her vivacious, warm personality, she would soon have scores of new friends. These people were her own age, shared the same interests. They would open up a whole world to her—one in which Grey regretfully acknowledged that he wouldn't belong. There was only one thing left for him to do.

Only it wasn't easy.

Thursday, after giving the matter some heavy-duty thought, Grey had felt downright noble deciding to

step aside for a man who would be far better suited to
someone like Meghan O'Day. There would soon be
several vying for her attention and Grey couldn't
blame them. It would be all too easy for him to fall in
love with her himself.

Meghan was sunshine and bright colors. Unfortunately, Grey's world was colored in black and white.
He was staid; she was effervescent—the embodiment
of warmth and femininity. And he was nothing more
than an ivory-tower professor, secure in his own world
and unwilling to venture far into another.

No. As difficult as it seemed now, it was better for
them both if he stepped out of her life before either of
them was badly hurt.

His feelings now, however, with the lonely week-
end facing him were far less admirable. He might be
doing the noble thing, but he didn't feel nearly as good
about it.

It was damn hard to release a ray of sunshine. In
fact, it was far more difficult than he ever imagined it
would be. Meghan O'Day was someone very sweet
and very special who drifted in and out of his life,
leaving him forever marked by their all-to-brief en-
counter.

A cold sensation of regret lapped over him. First, he
would phone Meghan and cancel their date for Saturday, and then he'd contact Pamela Riverside. Stiff
and exceedingly formal, Pamela was far more com-
patible with him. If nothing more, they understood
each other. And if he wasn't the least bit attracted to
her, well, there were other things in life that made up
for passion and excitement.

Feeling slightly guilty to be using Pamela to forget one sweet Irish miss with eyes as blue as turquoise jewels, Grey reached for the phone.

Meghan was busy folding clothes when her telephone pealed. Humming softly, she walked around the corner and lifted the receiver off the hook.

"Yo," she greeted cheerfully, easily falling into the greetings her brothers used so often. Meghan was in a marvelous mood. Life was going so well, lately. She'd missed seeing Grey on Wednesday and had felt badly about that, but by the time she'd left The Hub, she was shocked by how late it was. There hadn't even been time to run over and say hello.

"Meghan."

"Grey," she whispered on the end of happy sigh. "It's so good to hear from you. There's so much to tell you I don't know where to start," she said with a rush of excitement. "First of all, I'm sorry about the other day. I met someone while registering and we ended up having coffee with a couple of others, and the time slipped away without my even realizing it."

"I'm phoning about Saturday night," he announced brusquely.

"Oh, Grey, I'm really pleased you asked me to attend this cocktail party with you. Nervous, too, if you want the truth. You never did say how formal it was."

"Meghan," he said tightly. "Something's come up, and I'm afraid I'm going to have to cancel Saturday night."

"Oh." Meghan knew she'd been chattering, and immediately shut up.

"I apologize if this has caused you any inconvenience."

Grey sounded so formal that Meghan wasn't sure how to respond. "It's no problem. Don't worry about it."

"Good."

A short awkward silence followed, and Meghan decided the best thing to do was to ignore Grey's bad mood. "Oh, before I forget, Mom wanted me to ask you to dinner again next Sunday. Dad's eager to play chess again and the boys suggested you wear jeans so they won't have to worry about you ruining your suit pants."

"Meghan..."

"Grey, just wear what you're most comfortable in, and don't worry about my brothers."

"I won't be able to make it," he stated flatly. "Please extend my regrets to your family."

"All right," she replied wishing she knew what was wrong.

"I see that it's about time for you to leave for work," he said next, clearly wanting to end the conversation.

Meghan's gaze bounced to the face of her watch. "I've got a few minutes yet. Grey, is something the matter? You don't sound anything like yourself."

"I'm perfectly fine."

"It's not your health that concerns me, but your attitude."

"Yes, well," he said gruffly, "I've been doing a good deal of thinking over the last few days. It seems to me that since you're going to be attending Friends that it wouldn't do at all for us to keep dating each other."

An argument sprang to her lips, but she quickly swallowed it. It was clear from the tone of his voice that his mind was made up and that nothing she could say would change it. The disappointment was enough to make her want to cry.

"I understand." She didn't, but that wasn't what Grey wanted to hear. He was giving her the brush-off and trying to do it in the most tactful way possible.

"We'll still see each other every now and again," he continued in the same unemotional tone as though it didn't matter to him one way or the other. "In fact it'll be unavoidable, since both your classes are in the same building as the ones I'm teaching."

Meghan wondered how he knew that. She hadn't even told him which classes she'd registered for. It was apparent he'd done a bit of detective work and had sought out the information himself.

"Yes, I suppose that it will be inevitable, won't it?"

"You're going to do very well at Friends, Meghan. If you have any problems, I want you to feel free to contact me. I'll be happy to do whatever I can to help."

"Thank you."

"Goodbye, Meghan."

The words had a final ring to them that echoed over the wire like shouts against a canyon wall.

"Goodbye, Grey," she whispered. By the time she replaced the telephone receiver, her stomach felt as if a concrete block had settled there.

Chapter Seven

Meghan's arms were loaded with books when she stepped into the ivy-covered brick faculty building. The directory in the entrance listed Grey's office as being on the third floor.

With doubts pounding against her breast like a demolition ball, she stepped into the elevator. The ride up seemed to stretch into eternity. It had been two weeks since Meghan had last talked to Grey and her mind stumbled and tripped over what she planned to say. She didn't know if she was doing the right thing in approaching him like this, but she found the persistent silence between them intolerable. Men had come briefly into her life in the past, but none had mattered more to her than Grey. She found accepting his rejection of her both painful and nerve-racking.

"May I help you?" a middle-aged woman who sat behind an electric typewriter asked when Meghan entered the series of offices. Apparently several professors shared the same person, who acted as both receptionist and secretary.

"Yes, please," Meghan answered, smiling broadly. "I'm here to see Professor Carlyle."

Frowning, the gray-haired secretary leaned forward and leafed through the appointment book. "Is he expecting you?"

"No. If he's busy I could come back when it's more convenient."

The woman gave Meghan a sharp look. "Professor Carlyle is always busy," she intoned. "Tell me your name and I'll ask if he'll see you."

By this time Meghan was convinced she was making a terrible mistake. She seemed to be shaking from the inside out. Dropping in on Grey like this, with such a flimsy excuse, would only complicate an already complex relationship.

"My dear girl, I don't have all day. Your name."

"Meghan O'Day," she answered crisply, then hurried to add, "Listen, I think perhaps it would be better if I came back another time—"

Before she could say anything more, the receptionist had pushed down the intercom switch and announced to Grey that Meghan was outside his office. Almost immediately afterward, a door opened and Grey stood not more than ten feet from her.

"Meghan."

His gaze revealed a wealth of emotion: surprise, delight, regret, doubt. Not knowing which one to respond to first, she forced a smile and said, "I hope I'm not interrupting anything important." She should be more concerned about making an utter fool of herself, she decided, but it was too late to do anything else now but proceed full steam ahead. She pasted a smile

on her face and met his look, praying he wouldn't read
the tumult boiling just beneath the surface.

"You're not interrupting anything. Come in,
please." He stepped aside in order to admit her to his
office. Meghan walked into the compact room and sat
in a leather chair that was angled toward the huge
mahogany desk. Grey's office was almost exactly the
way she'd pictured it would be—meticulous in every
detail. Certificates and honors lined one wall, and
bookcases the other two. Behind his desk was a huge
picture window that gave an unobstructed view of the
campus below.

Shelf upon shelf of literary works were cramped together on the bookcases so that there wasn't a single
inch of space available. In other circumstances,
Meghan would have loved to examine his personal li-
brary.

"I suppose I should have called for an appointment first," she said, avoiding eye contact with him,
"but I decided to stop by on the spur of the moment
on my way back from the bookstore." She glanced
down at the load of textbooks in her arms.

By this time, Grey was seated in the swivel chair behind his desk.

"I'll admit this is a surprise. It's been what, now—
two weeks since we last talked?"

Two weeks, three days and four hours, Meghan
tallied mentally. "It's been about two weeks, I guess,"
she responded, hoping she didn't look half as nervous as she felt. Her stomach was in complete tur-
moil. She tightened her arms around the load of
books, holding them against her breast as though she
expected Grey to hurl something at her, which was

completely ridiculous. Now that she was here, she was convinced she'd made a drastic mistake.

Grey looked at her, waiting.

"It's been really cold lately, hasn't it? I feel we're going to be in for a harsh winter."

"Yes, it has been."

His look told her he had better things to do than discuss the weather. "I was on the campus to pick up my textbooks," she tried again.

He nodded, reminding her that she'd already told him that.

"How have you been, Meghan?"

"Good. Really good." Her response was eager and she scooted to the edge of her seat. "And you?"

"Fine, just fine."

Not knowing how else to proceed, she said, "I thought I'd take two classes this first time, since it's been so many years since I was in school.... I guess I already told you that, didn't I?"

"Yes, I believe you mentioned that before." A heavy silence followed until Grey asked, "How's your family?"

"They're fine. Mom's busy preparing for Thanksgiving." Her grip tightened all the more around the books until the inside of her arms ached from the unnecessary pressure.

A pulsating stillness followed. They'd exhausted the small talk and there was nothing left for Meghan to do but state the reason for her visit, which at best would sound terribly feeble.

"I've been coming to a reading group the last couple of Fridays here on campus," she began, forcing some enthusiasm into her voice. "I was thinking that you might like to join us sometime."

"I appreciate the fact you thought of me, but no," he said crisply.

She hadn't really expected him to accept her invitation, but she hadn't anticipated that his answer would be quite so abrupt. He hadn't even taken time to give the suggestion any thought. "I know you'd like the others," she felt obliged to add. "They share your views on a lot of subjects; they're thoughtful and intelligent and not nearly as opinionated as me." That was only a half-truth, but she was getting desperate.

"I don't have the time for it," he added starkly.

"I know you don't.... I should have realized that." She stood suddenly, with her heart pounding so fast and furiously, she was certain her ribs would soon crack.

"Meghan?"

"It was wrong to have come here. I'm sorry, Grey." As quickly as she could propel her legs, she stormed out of his office. If this were happening in a movie instead of real life, the elevator would have been open and ready to usher her away from the embarrassing scene. Naturally it wasn't, and she didn't have the time or patience to stand still for it.

"Meghan, wait!"

She couldn't. She should never had come to him like this. If making a fool of herself wasn't enough, tears filled her eyes—which added to her humiliation. If he saw them it would be that much worse.

Somehow she made it to the stairway, yanking open the door as hard as she could and vaulting down the stairs, taking two at a time until she feared she would stumble if she didn't slow down. Grey called her one last time, but she was forever grateful that he didn't try to follow her.

* * *

"The party at table twenty-two is waiting for his check," Sherry said as she brushed past Meghan that night at Rose's Diner.

"I've got it right here," Meghan replied, thanking her friend with a grin. She didn't know where her mind was tonight, but she'd felt sluggish and out of sorts all evening. On second thought, she did know where her mind was, but thinking about Grey was nonproductive and too damn painful. She paused and checked through the slips in her apron pocket and took the coffeepot with her as she delivered the tab to table twenty-two.

"Are you sure I can't talk you into a piece of pie?" she asked the elderly gentleman who was waiting there. "Rose's pecan is the special of the month."

"No, thanks," he said, patting his extended belly. "Rose's cooking has already filled me to the gills." He chuckled at his own joke and reached for his check.

Meghan went around the room refilling coffee cups when Sherry strolled past her a second time. "Don't look now, but trouble with a capital P just strolled in."

"Who?"

"Your professor friend," Sherry whispered, giving her a look that suggested Meghan had been working too many hours lately.

"Oh, great," Meghan groaned. She didn't want to face Grey—not after their disastrous confrontation earlier in the day.

"He requested your section, too."

"Sherry," Meghan pleaded, gripping her co-worker's forearm, "wait on him for me. Please, I can't. I just can't."

"Yes, you can!"

"I thought you were my friend."

"I am," she said, looking Meghan straight in the eye. "That's why I'm going to insist as assistant manager that you wait on your own customer. Some day you'll thank me for this."

"There'll be air-conditioning in hell before I do," she told her friend, her teeth clenched.

Sherry giggled and Meghan reached for a water glass and a menu to deliver to Grey's table. Once more, she noted, he sat in the booth by the window. A book lay open on the tabletop and he was intently reading, which meant he wasn't paying any attention to her. That was just as well.

As unobtrusively as possible, Meghan set down the water glass and menu and walked away. From out of the corner of her eye, she watched as Grey briefly picked up the plastic-coated menu and scanned its offerings. Either he made up his mind quickly or he wasn't particularly hungry, because he set it aside no more than a second or two after looking it over. His novel didn't seem to be holding his attention, either, because he closed that and pushed it away. His brow was pleated, his look brooding.

Meghan gave him an additional three minutes before she approached his table, her tablet in her hand. "Are you ready to order."

"Why did you run out of my office today?"

"The special is excellent this evening," she announced, ignoring his question. "Liver and onions—which I'm sure is one of your personal favorites."

"Meghan, please." He removed his horn-rimmed glasses, tucked them inside his jacket pocket and stared up at her.

Her eyelids drifted closed as embarrassment burned through her. "Pecan pie is the special of the month."

"I don't give a damn about the pie," he said force-fully, causing several patrons to glance in his direction. Grey smiled apologetically and added softly, "But I care about you."

Her eyes shot open. In his office, she'd felt inane and foolish, but now she was furious. "You care about me?" she echoed with disbelief.

"It's true."

She rolled her eyes. "Oh, please, spare me. You broke our date two weeks ago and I haven't heard from you since. Believe me, Professor Carlyle, I got your message—loud and clear."

"I—"

"You gave me a polite, educated brush-off in what I'm sure you felt was the kindest way possible. I can't say that I blame you. After all, you're a lofty professor and I'm nothing more than a waitress with a love for the classics. You're educated and brilliant. I'm simply not good enough for the likes of you."

Anger flared into his eyes, sparking them a bright blue. "You couldn't be more wrong."

Meghan doubted that, and sucked in a steadying breath before continuing in a sarcastic tone. "Hey, don't worry about it. I'm a big girl," she returned flippantly. "I can accept the fact you don't want to see me again."

"Then why were you at my office this afternoon?"

Meghan's mouth made troutlike movements as her mind staggered to come up with a plausible explanation. "Yes...well...that was a tactical error." Then she remembered she'd had an excuse for being there—all right, not a very profound one, but a reason. "I honestly thought you might enjoy joining the reading group," she claimed righteously, holding her head high.

Grey's gaze scanned the diner. "I can see that an explanation is going to be far more complicated than I thought. How much longer before you're off work?"

It was on the tip of her tongue to inform him he could wait all night and it wouldn't do any good because she had no intention of talking to him—ever. But that would have been a lie. As much as she longed to salvage her pride by suggesting he take a flying leap into the Arkansas River, Meghan wanted desperately to talk to him. She'd been utterly miserable for the past two weeks, missing Grey more than she'd thought it was possible to yearn for anyone she'd known so briefly. It was as if all the expectation had gone out of her life; and with it, all the fun and excitement.

"Another half hour. Would you like a piece of pecan pie while you wait?"

"Do you have custard pie?"

A smile flirted with her lips—the first genuine one in weeks. She should have known Grey would prefer custard over pecan. "Yes. I'll bring you a piece of pie and tea," she said, knowing he favored tea over coffee.

"Thank you."

While Meghan was slicing the custard pie, Sherry strolled past her and remarked, "Well, my friend, from the looks of things, the temperature in hell is several degrees cooler." She moved on past, chortling as she went.

The last fifteen minutes of Meghan's shift seemed to drag by. Sherry let her go a few minutes early, and Meghan changed out of her uniform in record time.

Grey was waiting for her in the parking lot. "Do you want to talk at your apartment, or would you prefer coming to my place?"

"Yours," Meghan replied automatically

For some reason, Meghan had assumed Grey lived in an apartment near the university, but she was wrong. She followed him to a house, a very nice two-story brick one with a sharply inclined roof and two gables.

She walked in the front door, doing her best not to ogle. The interior was decorated in a combination of leather and polished wood. As his office had been, the walls of his living room were lined with shelf upon shelf of obviously well-read books.

"Go ahead and make yourself comfortable," he said, taking her coat from her and hanging it in the entryway closet. "Would you like some coffee?"

"Please." She followed him into the kitchen where all the appliances were black and the sink was made of stainless steel. Everything was in perfect order, reminding Meghan that her own kitchen looked like something out of the Twilight Zone. Her stomach rumbled and she placed a hand over her abdomen, silently commanding it to be quiet.

"You're hungry. Didn't you have dinner?"

She shrugged. "Actually, I wasn't in the mood for anything tonight." She'd been too depressed and miserable to think about anything as mundane as eating.

"Can I fix you a sandwich?"

"No, thanks," she returned, although the mere mention of food was enough to make her mouth salivate. Now that she had time to think about it, she was famished.

Grey pulled out a white cushioned stool with a wicker back for her to sit on while he busied himself with the coffee. He seemed to be composing his thoughts as he filled the coffee machine with water.

"I saw you in The Hub," he said as he opened the cupboard and took out two coffee cups. The dark liquid had just started to leak into the glass pot.

"When?" She'd only been there a handful of times.

His back was to her. "The day you registered for classes."

He seemed to place some importance on that fact that Meghan didn't seem to understand. "Yes, I was there."

"Making new friends?" he coaxed

"Yes. That was the day I met Eric Vogel and the others in the reading group."

"I see."

"*What* do you see?" Meghan pressed. He was using those same words again and in that identical tone of voice that she'd come to dread.

He turned around, his face as tight and constrained as his voice. "You and those other students looked right together."

She frowned. "I don't understand."

He gripped the edge of the counter behind him with his hands. "No, I don't suppose you do." His gaze studied the polished black-and-white checkered linoleum floor. "A whole new world is about to open up for you, Meghan," he said, smiling wryly. "You've devoted yourself to your family and your job since the time you finished high school. As soon as you start at the university, you're going to meet lots of new friends."

"Yes, I suppose I will." She still had no idea what he was getting at.

"What I'm trying to tell you, and apparently doing a poor job of it, is that you could have any man you wanted."

Meghan was so shocked that for a minute she didn't speak. "Grey, honestly, you seemed to have overestimated my charms." She couldn't very well announce that the only man who interested her was him! "And even if what you're saying is true, and it isn't, what has it got to do with you and me?"

"Everything." He looked surprised that she would even raise the question.

Meghan couldn't believe what she was hearing. Her stomach gurgled again and she pressed her hand harder against her midriff. "Let me see if I understand your reasoning—"

"There's nothing to understand. I don't want to stand in your way."

"Stand in my way?" she echoed, and jumped off the stool. Her stomach was churning and growling again, making her all the more unreasonable. "Oh, shut up," she cried.

Grey looked positively shocked.

"I wasn't talking to you."

"Is there someone else here I don't see?"

"My stomach won't be quiet."

"Dammit, Meghan, why didn't you accept the sandwich I offered?"

"Because I'm too furious with you!" She was pacing now, lost in a free-fall of thoughts and emotions.

"I'll make you something to eat and you'll feel better," he suggested calmly.

"Stand in my way of what?" she pressed, ignoring his offer of food.

"Of finding someone special like Eric or any one of the others. I noticed how interested in you they all seemed to be. Frankly I couldn't blame them. You're warm and witty, and—"

"Miserable."

"I know you're hungry," he persisted, opening his refrigerator. "I'll have a sandwich ready for you any minute." Already he was gathering the fixings on the kitchen counter.

"I don't want a sandwich," she told him, clenching and unclenching her hands at her side.

"Soup, then?"

"You might have asked me how I felt before making that kind of decision. What gives you the right to decide who I should and shouldn't see? Don't you think it would have been better to discuss this with me first? I've been miserable, Grey, and all because you thought Eric and I looked good together. By the way, Eric's fiancée may think differently about that."

He stopped and turned to face her, a frown creasing his brow. "I have the distinct feeling we're discussing two entirely different subjects here. I thought we were discussing making a sandwich."

"A sandwich? We're talking about my life!"

"Oh." He looked both flustered and uneasy.

"Are you really so insensitive?"

"Actually," he said, boldly meeting her gaze, "*insecure* would be a more appropriate word. I didn't realize you'd been hurt by this until today when you came to my office. Frankly, I was more than a little surprised. I assumed you'd start dating any one of the others and quickly forget me."

"Both insensitive *and* insecure, then," she whispered.

A hush followed her statement. Meghan watched, standing as stiff as a new recruit in front of a drill sergeant, waiting. Her chin was elevated to a haughty angle.

Grey had revealed no faith in her or the attraction she felt for him—none. He'd seen her as a flighty teenager easily swayed by the charms and attention of another.

"Will an apology suffice?" he asked after an elongated moment, meeting her look.

"An apology and a sandwich would be an excellent start. Anything beyond that will need to be negotiated separately."

"Meghan, there's no need for you to be so nervous," Grey said as he pulled his car into a parking space outside Dr. Browning's home.

Grey had insisted she attend this cocktail party with him at the elegant home of the president of Friends University. Meghan had hoped that Grey would introduce her to his friends gradually, but he claimed this would be much easier. Easier for him, perhaps, but hell on her nerves.

"What, me worried?" she joked, doing her best to disguise her nervousness. Grey may have insisted she attend this party with him, but she doubted he would include her in another. Her heart was in her throat, and she hadn't said more than a dozen words to him from the minute he'd picked her up at the apartment. During the half-hour drive to Dr. Browning's home, it was all Meghan could do to keep from wringing her hands.

"You're as pale as a sheet." He reached for her hand, squeezing it reassuringly. "Everyone's going to love you, so stop worrying."

"Right," she said, forcing some eagerness into her voice. She'd never dreaded a party more. In the beginning, she'd been pleased and excited that Grey had asked her to accompany him; it had meant so much at the time. But now Meghan would have done just about anything to come up with a plausible excuse to get out of this formal gathering. Her mind kept repeating the line about fools rush in where angels fear to tread.

Grey came around to her side of the car and opened the passenger door.

Meghan tightened her fingers around her small evening bag and sucked in her breath. "Grey, I know this is going to sound crazy, but I feel a terrible headache coming on.... Maybe it would be best if you drove me home."

"Nonsense. I'll ask Joan to get you an aspirin."

An over-the-counter drug wasn't going to help her, but arguing with him wouldn't do any good, either.

"You're sure about this?" She felt she had to ask him that and give him the opportunity to back out gracefully before she said or did anything that would embarrass them both.

"Positive," he returned confidently.

Meghan's fingers felt like blocks of ice. The chill extended up her arms and seemed to center someplace between her belly and her heart.

"Before we go inside would you do something for me?" she asked hurriedly.

"You mean other than take you home?" he chided gently, smiling at her.

"Yes."

"Anything, Meghan. What do you need?"

She was sitting sideways in the car, half in and half out, wondering if she'd lost her mind.

"Meghan?"

"I . . . I don't know what I want," she whispered.

"You're cold?"

She nodded so hard, she feared she would ruin her hair, and she'd spent hours carefully weaving every strand into place to make an elaborate French braid. It seemed exactly the way she should style it for this evening, although she rarely wore her shoulder-length curls any way except loose.

"I think I know what you need," he said, and looked over his shoulder before leaning forward slightly and planting his hands on her shoulders.

Meghan blinked her eyes a couple of times, wondering at this game, when Grey lowered his mouth to hers in a soft, gentle kiss that spoke of solace more than passion. He pressed his lips to hers in the briefest of contacts.

Meghan sighed and braced her hands against his forearms, needing something to root herself in reality. Was this Grey holding her? The same man who would normally frown upon kissing where there was a chance of their being seen?

He kissed her a third time and then a fourth, as though a sample weren't nearly enough to satisfy him and he needed much, much more.

When he lifted his head, she could feel the color returning to her face and she was beginning to experience the faint stirrings of warmth seep back into her blood.

"There. How do you feel now?"

"Almost kissed."

He frowned slightly. "I suppose that was unfair, but I couldn't think of any other way to get some rosiness back into you cheeks. You looked as if you were about to faint. Are you ready now?"

"As ready as I'll ever be."

He discharged his breath and linked his fingers with hers. "Just be yourself, Meghan. There's nothing to worry about. Try to enjoy tonight."

"I know I will," she murmured, although she knew that would be impossible.

Together, hand in hand, they strolled up to the large Colonial-style home of the university president.

Nearly immediately, Meghan realized her fears were mostly unfounded. The first people she met were President Browning and his wife, Joan. From the moment she was introduced to her, Meghan liked Joan Browning, who was warm and personable—gracious to the marrow of her bones.

"Greyson's mentioned you several times," Joan stated while the two men engaged in brief conversation. "Both John and I have been looking forward to meeting you for weeks."

Meghan did a good job of disguising her surprise. "Thank you for including me this evening."

"Nonsense. Thank you for coming."

They moved into the house and Grey slipped his arm around Meghan's waist. "There, that wasn't so bad, was it?"

"No," she had to agree. Surprisingly, it had been rather painless. She'd like Joan Browning, who had gone out of her way to make sure that Meghan felt comfortable and welcome.

"Are you ready to meet a few of the others?" Grey asked.

"Not until I've had some champagne," she said lightly, knowing the alcohol would help her relax. One glass was her limit, but she knew some of her nervousness would disappear with that.

Obligingly Grey fetched them each a glassful of champagne, leaving Meghan for a few short moments. He returned and smiled down at her with both warmth and humor.

"Have I told you how lovely you look tonight?"

"About four times, and I appreciated hearing it every time."

He chuckled. "I feel fortunate to have you with me this evening."

"I'm the one who should be saying that," Meghan whispered, knowing all too well that *she* was the fortunate one. "Grey, who's that woman sitting across the room from us?" she asked, when she couldn't ignore her any longer. "She's been sending daggers my way from the moment we walked in. Do you know her?"

Meghan felt Grey tense. "Yes, well..." He paused and cleared his throat. "I'm sure you're imagining things."

"I'm not. Who is she?" Meghan prodded

"That's Dr. Pamela Riverside." He was clearly uneasy. He finished the last of his champagne in one swallow and set the tall thin glass aside.

"I think it's time you introduced us, don't you?" Meghan asked, realizing that the champagne had given her the courage necessary to suggest such a thing.

"Frankly, no."

Chapter Eight

Hello, I'm Meghan O'Day," Meghan said, greeting the woman with steel-blue eyes who'd been glaring at her for the past half hour. If Grey wasn't going to make the introductions, then she would see to it herself. The minute Meghan had been free to do so, she'd slipped away from Grey, who'd been engaged in conversation.

"I'm Dr. Pamela Riverside," the other woman said stiffly, holding on to her champagne glass as though she expected it to protect her against alien forces. "I... I'm a colleague of Dr. Carlyle's."

"I assumed that you were."

"Greyson's never mentioned me?" the other woman asked softly, lowering her gaze, looking vulnerable and desperately trying to hide it.

"Grey may have, but I don't recall that he did," Meghan said, after searching through her memory and drawing a blank as far as Dr. Riverside went. From his reaction earlier, Meghan was almost certain that Grey hadn't said a word about his colleague. In fact, it seemed obvious that he was doing everything he could to keep the two of them apart.

"I didn't think he had," Pamela responded in a hurt voice that trembled just a little.

Meghan's pulse started to accelerate at an alarming rate. The thoughts that flashed through her mind seared her conscience. If Dr. Riverside was shooting daggers in Meghan's direction, then there was probably a very good reason. Perhaps Grey had jilted the other woman, and had left her with a battered and bleeding heart. The more Meghan studied the female professor, the more she realized she wore the look of a woman done wrong by her man. She was taller than Meghan by several inches, and thin to the point of being gaunt. Her dark hair was styled in a severe chignon that did little to soften the sharp contours of her cheeks and eyes. Without much effort, she could have been appealing and attractive, but her style of clothing was outdated and she didn't even bother with lipstick or eye shadow.

"Actually, there isn't any reason why Grey should have said anything about me," Pamela continued, looking more miserable by the minute. "He's never been anything but the perfect gentleman with me. If I were to tell you anything different, it would be a lie."

"I don't suppose he mentioned me, then, either," Meghan muttered. Grey had always been "the perfect gentleman" with her, as well. Meghan doubted that he would ever be anything else.

"No, I can't say that he did comment on you," Dr. Riverside confirmed brusquely, looking pleased to be telling Meghan as much.

That didn't help Meghan to feel any better. In fact she felt downright discouraged. She wasn't so naive to believe there hadn't been women in Grey's past. He might even be involved with someone now, although she doubted it.

"Actually, there isn't any reason he should tell you about me, either," Meghan admitted with some reluctance.

The beginnings of a smile flirted at the edges of Pamela's mouth. "That's where you're wrong."

"Wrong?" Meghan didn't like the sound of this.

"He didn't have to tell me anything about you. I knew almost from the first."

Meghan wondered briefly exactly *what* it was the other woman knew. "I'm not sure I understand," she said, wishing now that she hadn't refused a second glass of champagne. This convoluted conversation wasn't making much sense.

"By my calculations, I'd guess that you and Grey started going out the last part of October."

Meghan nodded, confirming the other woman's conjecture. She wasn't sure how Pamela Riverside had known that, and wasn't convinced she even wanted to know. Meghan was about to ask another question, when Grey casually strolled up and joined them.

"Pamela," he said as a means of greeting her, dipping his head slightly. He held himself as stiff as a freshly-starched shirt collar, his hands buried deep in his pockets. "I can see you've met Meghan O'Day."

"We introduced ourselves," Meghan explained.

Grey's deep blue eyes revealed his disapproval, which surprised Meghan all the more. From everything he'd been saying and doing, it was obvious he didn't want Meghan to have anything to do with his colleague. But his efforts to keep them apart only served to pique Meghan's interest.

"There are some people I'd like you to meet," Grey stated possessively slipping his arm around Meghan's waist. "If you'll excuse us, Pamela."

"Of course," Pamela murmured, but some of the stiffness returned to her voice. "It was nice meeting you, Meghan."

"You, too," she answered, genuinely meaning it. "We'll talk again soon."

"I'd like that."

Grey tensed and then led Meghan away. Although it could have been her imagination, it seemed that he was unnecessarily eager to remove her from the other woman's presence.

An hors d'oeuvre table had been set up, and several of the guests were milling around there, talking. Meghan recognized a couple of professors from her few visits to the Friends campus, but the others were all strangers.

It soon became apparent that there wasn't anyone in particular Grey meant to introduce her to and that he'd used the ploy as an excuse to get Meghan away from Dr. Riverside. He eased them into line and handed Meghan a small plate and napkin.

Once they'd served themselves, Grey escorted her into the family room. Only one other couple had opted to sit there and they were on the other side of the room, deeply involved in their own conversation. Grey directed Meghan to the sofa, sitting next to her but twisting around so that his back was braced against the armrest and he could look at her.

"I suppose you're full of questions now," he muttered disparagingly.

"No," Meghan fibbed. Her head was buzzing, wanting answers, but she'd intended to ask them in her own good time.

"There never has been anything between me and Pamela, no matter what she told you," he volunteered, his voice elevated and sharp. "Never."

"She didn't suggest that there was."

Grey sagged with relief as the tension slackened between his shoulder blades. "Pamela's ripe for marriage and she's going to make some man an excellent wife—but not me!"

He said this with such vehemence that Meghan nearly swallowed her cracker whole. "I see," she said, not meeting his look.

Grey paused and studied her through eyes that had narrowed suspiciously. "I understand now why you dislike it so much when I say that," he mumbled, clearly all the more troubled. "Exactly what did she tell you?"

"Nothing much." There hadn't been time.

He paused and briefly rubbed the back of his neck. "Pamela and I have been part of the university's literature department for several years. We've worked closely together, and I suppose it's only natural for her to assume certain things. Our backgrounds are similar, and through no fault of our own we've often been coupled together." He rearranged the appetizers on his plate, shifting them around as if doing so was vital to their discussion.

"She's in love with you."

Grey's head shot up so fast, Meghan wondered if he'd strained his neck. "She told you that?"

"She didn't need to. I realized it almost from the moment we walked in here tonight."

"I've never done anything to encourage her, Meghan. I swear to you that's true. We've been thrown together socially for years, and I suspect that several of the university staff have assumed that the two of us were romantically involved. But that isn't true, I promise you it isn't."

"Okay," she said, taking a bite of a cheese-stuffed cherry tomato. "Hmm, this is delicious. Are you going to eat yours?"

Grey's gaze was disbelieving, as though he couldn't quite believe that she could comment on an hors d'oeuvre when the fate of their budding relationship hung in the balance. "You mean you aren't angry?"

"Should I be?"

"No," he claimed fervently, pushing his hand through his hair until his fingers made deep grooves in the dark mane. "There's absolutely no reason for you to be!"

"Then I'm not angry."

"You're sure?"

"Positive." She reached for the cheese-stuffed cherry tomato on his plate. If he didn't want it, she did. "As far as I can see, there isn't any reason to be jealous, either. So I won't be."

His jaw sagged open as though he expected an argument and was almost disappointed when Meghan didn't give him one.

"Grey, you don't have to do this," Meghan urged, her gaze holding his. She still had trouble believing that he'd allowed her two youngest brothers to talk him into this craziness. It was the Wednesday before Thanksgiving and Meghan had a free evening in the middle of the week, which was rare indeed. Sherry had given her the night off to compensate for having her work on the holiday.

"To be honest, I'm not quite sure how they talked me into this, either," Grey replied, chuckling lightly, "but it's something I'd like to do—especially since you're able to come with us."

He parked his car in front of her family home and the minute he did, Chad and Danny burst out the door as if they couldn't get away fast enough.

"It isn't like the boys never get to go to the movies," Meghan reminded him. "They should never have phoned you and asked you to take them."

"From what Chad said, they needed someone over seventeen to accompany them because this movie has a high degree of violence."

"Brian's over seventeen."

"He's busy."

"And you're not?"

"Meghan—" he reached for her hand "—I want to do this. I haven't been to a movie in years, and this was the perfect excuse to see *Chainsaw Murder, Part Three*."

"But you didn't see the first two, and if you had, I'm fairly certain you wouldn't be interested in the sequel. In fact, I'm absolutely positive you're going to hate this movie."

"Let me be the judge of that."

"Don't say that I didn't warn you." If what Grey said was true and he hadn't been to a movie in years, then he was about to receive the shock of his life. Horror films weren't what they were in Hitchcock's day. There were blood and guts and gore enough to affect even the most hard-hearted.

"Hi, Professor," Danny greeted as he leaped into the back seat of Grey's car with the enthusiasm of a herd of charging elephants. "We're really glad you're taking Chad and me to the movies, aren't we, Chad?"

"Yeah." Chad's enthusiasm wasn't nearly as keen as his brother's. "But I didn't know Meghan was coming along," he added, eyeing his sister skeptically.

"I felt I should, since you two blackmailed Grey into this evening's outing. Whose bright idea was it to call him, anyway?"

"Danny's," Chad shouted.

"Chad's," Danny retorted in the same loud voice as his brother's.

"I don't mind," Grey insisted, reminding Meghan a second time that he'd been a willing victim of her brothers' schemes.

"But I saw the previews to this movie," Meghan told him. "It's really bloody and violent."

"I can stand a little blood."

"Yeah, so can I," Chad said with the eagerness only a teenager could understand.

"Me, too," Danny chimed in.

"Well, as long as it isn't my own blood, I guess I'm outvoted," Meghan murmured, accepting her fate.

Chad released a huge sigh of relief. "I was afraid when I saw Meghan that she was going to force us to go see something else, like a love story. Yuck!"

"It could be worse," Danny muttered under his breath. "Meghan could have insisted we see a musical."

"Come on, you guys, it's not that bad." Grey was so good to her brothers. This wasn't the first time he'd gone out of his way to take them somewhere. Her own mother was half in love with him herself, and it was little wonder. Grey had been to the house twice, and each time he'd brought her roses and faithfully mailed her thank-you cards for having him over for dinner. If Grey had set out to win her family, he couldn't have done a better job. They were all as crazy about him as she was. In some ways it troubled Meghan, the way he catered to them all. But it was only natural that, as an only child, he would be attracted to her fun-loving family. He worked so hard to be a part of them—playing chess with her father, subjecting himself to football with her younger brothers. Deep inside her heart, Meghan was thrilled that he cared enough to strive to be one of them. Yet a small, doubting part of herself worried that it was her family that Grey was attracted to, and that being with her was just a bonus. As much as possible, however, Meghan tried to ignore the negative thought.

Grey found a suitable parking place at the Wichita Mall and escorted them into the cinema.

"We don't have to stay with you two, do we?" Danny asked, once he was loaded down with popcorn and a drink. "We'd look like a bunch of wimps if we had to sit with you guys."

"We *can* sit on our own, can't we?" Chad repeated his brother's concern.

"Sit where we can see you, that's all I ask," Meghan answered for Grey.

"Why?" Chad and Danny demanded together. "We aren't little kids, you know."

"In case something happens and we have to leave early, I want to know where you are so I don't have to rove the aisles to find you," she insisted.

The boys rolled their eyes and then glared at each other as though they suspected Meghan had been talking to their mother too frequently. If they had any further protests, they chose to forget them and hurried off on their own.

Carrying the popcorn and drinks, Grey paused at the back of the theater. "Is there anyplace special you want to sit?" he asked Meghan.

"Near the back, so when the blood and guts start flowing, I can made a quick escape." Grey chose seats in the second to the last row. In contrast, Chad and Danny were in the third row from the front so that the huge white screen loomed in front of them. If they were any closer, their noses would have touched it. Neither one, it seemed, wanted to miss any of the gory details. Once seated, Meghan's two brothers twisted around and when they saw their sister, gave a short, perfunctory wave.

When Grey seemed sure Meghan was comfortable, he handed her a box of popcorn. She shoved a handful of kernels into her mouth, chewing as fast as possible. She figured she should eat what she could now, because once the movie started she wouldn't have the stomach for it.

The lights dimmed and Meghan held her breath while the credits started to roll across the screen. The minute the violence started, Meghan covered her eyes and scooted so far down in her seat that her forehead was level with the backs of the chairs in front of her.

"Meghan," Grey whispered. "Are you all right?"

"No."

He scrunched down, too, so his that face was even with her own. "Do you want to leave?"

"Chad and Danny would never forgive me." She kept her eyes closed. "Is the girl dead yet?"

"The girl?"

"The one in the movie," Meghan whispered heatedly. Who else could she possible mean, for heaven's sake?

"Yeah, and her friend, too."

"Oh, thank goodness." Meghan uncovered her eyes and sat upright. "I'm going to have nightmares all week because of this stupid movie."

Grey straightened, then looped his arm around her back, cupping her shoulder. "Does this help?"

She smiled into the darkness and nodded.

"And this?" Gently he pressed her head close to his shoulder.

"That's even better." Meghan leaned her head against the solid cushion of his chest as he shared his warmth and his strength with her. Only when she was so close to Grey could Meghan ignore the grisly details of the graphically played-out murder story.

Content, Meghan looked up at Grey and their gazes met in the dark. Grey gently smiled down at her, and the movie, at least for Meghan, faded into oblivion.

What surprised Meghan most was how much a smile from Grey could affect her. Her heart, which had been beating hard anyway, accelerated, stopped cold and then started up again. She longed for him to kiss her, and her eyes must have told him as much, yet she could feel Grey's resistance. Meghan couldn't blame him—she was asking for the absurd. They were in a crowded theater; anyone could see them.

"Meghan," he whispered.

"I know," she murmured, her eyes downcast. "Later."

"No," he growled softly. "Now." He bent his face toward hers, and his breath fanned her upturned face. Their lips met in the gentlest of kisses—velvet against satin, petal-soft, sweet, gentle, addictive.

Grey breathed in harshly and leaned his forehead against her own. "Sweet Meghan O'Day, the things you do to me."

A tornado could have descended on her at that moment, and Meghan wouldn't even have noticed. The mighty wind that would destroy everything in its path wouldn't have fazed her. Nothing could have compared to the rush of emotion that rocked through her. She was falling in love with Professor Greyson Carlyle—head over heels in love with him. Up to this point she'd been attracted to him, infatuated with him and challenged by the differences between them; but her feelings went beyond all that now. Some time after the cocktail party at President Browning's house and before tonight, she'd willingly surrendered her heart to this man. The precise time and place remained a mystery.

Grey kissed her one last time, and the kiss was long and thorough. Their lips clung to each other and when they broke apart, it was with heavy reluctance.

Meghan hardly noticed the remainder of the film. At several places in the movie the audience gasped at some gruesome sight, but all Meghan did was sigh and lean against Grey, soaking up his warmth.

When the film was finally over, light filled the theater. Meghan straightened and Grey disentangled his arms from around her.

"We might as well wait for the boys in the lobby," Grey suggested. He helped Meghan on with her coat after she stood.

Behind them, she heard two girls whispering.

"That *is* Professor Carlyle," came the first voice, clearly female.

"It can't be," returned the second, also feminine. "Old Stone Face? Think about it. Professor Carlyle never cracks a joke or hardly ever smiles. He just isn't the type to pay money to see this kind of movie. It couldn't possibly be the same man."

"I know you're right, Carrie, but I swear it looks just like him."

"He's got a woman with him, too. Someone young."

A short silence followed. Meghan was sure that Grey couldn't help overhearing the conversation any more than she could. Catching his gaze, she tried to reassure him with a timid smile, but if he saw it, he didn't respond.

"I read somewhere that everyone has a twin in this world," the whispering continued. "I bet that man's Professor Carlyle's twin."

"She's too young for him, don't you think?"

On the way out of the aisle, Grey kept his arm tucked around Meghan's waist. He stopped at the last row, paused and looked down at the two teenage girls, who remained sitting. They glared up at him, their mouths gaping open.

"Good evening, Carrie . . . Carol," he said evenly.

Both teens straightened in their seats as though they'd been caught doing something illegal. "Hello, Professor Carlyle."

"It's good to see you again, sir."

With his hand guiding Meghan at the base of her spine, he directed her into the lobby.

Meghan waited until they were near the exit doors before she spoke. "Greyson Carlyle, that was cruel and unusual punishment."

"Perhaps," he agreed, his smile noticeably forced.

Chad and Danny walked out of the main part of the theater looking as though they could hardly wait to see *Chainsaw Murder, Part Four*. Meghan cringed at the mere thought of having to sit through another sequel to the dreadful horror film. If Grey had any intention of saying anything more to her about what they'd overheard earlier, the chance was gone.

"Wasn't that rad?" Chad asked, looking to Grey for his approval. "Danny and I want to thank you for taking us—we probably wouldn't have been able to go if it hadn't been for you."

The comment was designed to cause Meghan to feel guilty for not being more willing to accompany her brothers to such important events, but she refused to be so much as tempted by the emotion. If it had been up to her, they would have gone to see a musical—and both Chad and Danny knew it.

"The movie was rad?" Grey repeated, arching his brows and glancing in Meghan's direction.

"Rad means cool, groovy—you know," Chad explained conversationally.

Grey nodded, his blue eyes serious. What humor shone there seemed forced. "Now that you mention it, I *do* know what that means. Banana splits are rad, aren't they? I wonder if you two boys would be game for one?"

"Are you nuts? We'd love it," Danny answered for them both.

"Grey, you're spoiling them," Meghan protested, but not too strenuously. She enjoyed watching Grey interact with the boys, and it was obvious they were equally fascinated with him.

"Oh, Meghan, don't ruin it for us. Grey's not spoiling us. He offered all on his own, without any coaxing."

"Yeah. We didn't even have to ask—" Danny tagged on his own feelings "—Grey's just being a pal."

"That's right," Grey said, and wrapped his arm around Meghan's shoulders.

He led the way outside, keeping Meghan close, but she felt him withdrawing even as he offered to take the boys out for dessert.

"From what I hear about your Uncle Harry," Grey said to Meghan, "I'm going to need all the friends I can find for tomorrow."

Meghan had nearly forgotten that her infamous uncle would be joining the O'Day family for the Thanksgiving festivities the following day. Uncle Harry was a known teaser, who delighted in saying and doing things that were sure to embarrass the younger generation. Usually he had a trick or two up his sleeve, and he delighted in fooling all the family members.

"I don't think you have much to worry about, Grey," Meghan assured him. "Uncle Harry's mellowed out the last several years."

"Does he play chess?"

"Not with my father," Meghan explained, chuckling. The only one brave enough to tackle Pat O'Day was the man whose arm was draped over her shoulder.

"What about football?"

"Loves it, as long it's on a screen and doesn't involve anything more than a few choice words of advice for the referees and coaches. You're in luck. He hasn't personally touched a football in years."

Grey nodded. "Then he sounds like my kind of man."

Following banana splits at the ice-cream parlor, Grey dropped Chad and Danny off at the house, stopping in briefly to say hello to Meghan's parents. Then he drove Meghan back to her apartment. He was unusually quiet the whole way there, and she longed to bring up the incident in the theater, but wasn't sure how. A couple of times she was tempted to make a joke of it, then decided it would be better if Grey mentioned the episode himself. She didn't know why Grey should be so troubled by it, but he obviously was. Their evening had been perfect until two of his students had recognized him and commented.

"You'll come up for coffee, won't you?" she invited, hoping that he would. Then at least there was the chance they would talk this matter out.

"You're not too tired?" he asked, then promptly yawned. He looked almost embarrassed as he placed his hand over his mouth.

"I'm fine. But from the look of it, you're exhausted."

"It's been a hectic week." He yawned a second time, looking chagrined. "Maybe I'd better just walk you to your door and say good-night there."

He escorted her to her apartment door and brushed his lips over hers in the briefest of kisses, leaving Meghan feeling frustrated and cheated.

"Good night."

"Good night, Grey. I'll see you tomorrow."

His answering smile was lame at best. Meghan bit into her bottom lip to keep from calling out for him to come back. Instead, she moved inside her apartment and plopped herself down on the sofa, letting her disappointment work its way through her.

The following morning when Meghan walked into her family home, she was immediately greeted with the pungent smells of sage and pumpkin-pie spices.

"Meghan, I'm glad you're here," her mother greeted and kissed her on the cheek. "Grey just phoned. He told me he tried to catch you, but apparently you'd just left the apartment."

Meghan dipped her finger into the whipped topping and promptly licked it, savoring the sweet taste. Her mother insisted upon using real cream in her recipes and not the imitation products that had become so popular over the years.

"Is Grey going to be late?" Meghan asked, examining the variety of dishes that lined the kitchen counter.

"No," her mother said sadly. "He called to give us his regrets. He won't be able to spend the day with us, after all. Apparently something's come up."

Chapter Nine

Something's come up?" Meghan echoed her mother's words, hardly able to believe what she'd heard. "What did Grey mean by that?"

"I don't know, princess, but he hardly sounded like his usual self." Her mother was busy whittling away on a huge pile of potatoes. Once they were peeled, she let them fall into a large pot of salted water.

Normally Meghan would have reached for a paring knife and lent a helping hand, but she was too upset. She started pacing the kitchen, her arms wrapped around her trim waist, her gaze centered on the ceiling while her thoughts collided in a wild tailspin. She should have guessed something like this would happen following the incident with two of Grey's students in the theater.

"I was afraid this would happen," she muttered, discouraged and disappointed—in both Grey and herself. She should have insisted they talk about what happened before he left her apartment.

"Did you and Grey have a falling-out, dear?" her mother asked, reaching for another potato.

"Not really." Meghan leaned her hip against the sink and appealed to her mother with her hands. "Do you think I'm too young for Grey?"

"Sweetheart, what I think is of little importance," she said matter-of-factly. "That's something that should be settled between you and Grey, not you and me."

"I know you're right." Meghan hesitated, then exhaled sharply, thinking it might help to discuss the matter with her mother. "Last night a couple of Grey's students were in the theater. They were whispering and we couldn't help overhearing what they said. Those girls seemed to think Grey was too old for me. Honestly, Mom, it doesn't bother me. Dad's eight years older than you and it's never been an issue."

"Seven and a half years," her father corrected as he sauntered into the kitchen. He reached inside the cupboard above the refrigerator and brought out a huge bag of salted peanuts.

"Don't be ruining your dinner, Patrick O'Day," Colleen warned, shaking her index finger at him.

"I won't, but a man's got to have some nourishment." He wrapped his arms around his wife's waist and nuzzled her neck. "You can't expect me to live on turkey and stuffing alone, you know."

"Oh, get away with you." Colleen chuckled and squirmed out of his embrace. "Dinner will be ready by one."

"We're eating early this year, aren't we?"

"I've got to be to work by three, Dad," Meghan reminded her father. She hesitated and glanced at the kitchen clock. If she hurried, there would be enough time for her to drive over to Grey's house and talk some reason into him. With any luck, she would be able to convince him to join her and the rest of her family at least for dinner, if not all day. To allow those two thoughtless students to ruin the holiday would be wrong, but the fact that Grey had allowed the matter to upset him to this extent troubled her even more.

"Mom," she said hurriedly. "Do you need my help in the kitchen, or can I leave you for a few minutes?"

"No, everything's under control—your Aunt Theresa's due any time. Are you going over to Grey's? Good—you convince him to come to dinner. Remember the way to a man's heart often leads through his stomach."

Smiling, Meghan nodded, not surprised that her mother had read her thoughts. "That sounds like a good idea," Colleen agreed, surprising Meghan. "Don't come back without him, you hear?"

"I won't." Meghan kissed her mother's cheek, appreciating her understanding. "I shouldn't be any more than an hour. Longer if he proves to be stubborn."

Colleen O'Day laughed softly. "Then I won't look for you for at least two hours."

All the way over to Grey's house, Meghan prepared her arguments. Her mother was right—more than right! Neither one of them could afford to allow what others thought to dictate their relationship. The instant she arrived, she planned on kissing Grey long and hard. *Then* he could tell her she was too young for him. The strategy had merit, and Meghan grinned, knowing full well that Grey wouldn't have a leg to stand on!

Smiling at this novel plan of attack, she parked her car on the street in front of his house. Excited now, she hurried up the stairs, rang the doorbell and waited impatiently.

"Meghan." Her name was issued on a rush of surprised pleasure when Grey opened the door.

"Now listen here, Greyson Carlyle, what's this about you not coming over for Thanksgiving dinner," she accused, her eyes flashing with mischief. "Mom gave me some flimsy excuse not even worth mentioning. I want to know exactly what you think you're doing, and I want to know right now." She punctuated each word by playfully poking a finger in his stomach. With each thrust, Grey took a step in reverse, his eyes wide and disbelieving.

"Meghan..."

He tried to get her to listen, but she wouldn't let him. "I can't believe you'd let what two students said disturb you this way. If you're worried about our age difference, then I dare you to take me in your arms. I challenge you to kiss me and then argue the point."

"Greyson, who is this woman?"

The sober, dry voice came from behind Grey, in the direction of the kitchen.

Stunned, Meghan looked beyond him to face an austere middle-aged woman with silver-white hair that was severely tucked away from her face. She wore a dark blue suit and black shoes—and no smile. Meghan blinked, certain she'd inadvertently run into Pamela Riverside's mother.

"Meghan O'Day, I'd like to introduce my mother, Dr. Frances Carlyle."

"How do you do, Dr. Carlyle?" Meghan said, the teasing laughter in her eyes wilting away under the solemn stare of the older woman. Meghan stepped forward and the two exchanged a brisk handshake. Her legs felt as if they'd turned to water and the size of the knot in her throat would have rivaled a golf ball.

"Are you a student of Greyson's?" his mother asked, her gaze boring holes into Meghan. Her tone wasn't openly unfriendly, but it lacked any real interest.

"No—we're friends," Meghan quickly explained.

"I see."

There was that phrase again. Meghan longed to share a knowing look with Grey, but she dared not.

"Mother was here waiting for me when I returned last night," Grey explained. He motioned toward the recliner, indicating that Meghan should take a seat. Apparently he noticed she was having trouble remaining in an upright position.

"Would you like some tea?" Frances Carlyle asked.

"Please." Meghan accepted, hoping that once Grey's mother had vacated the room, she could talk to him. She wished with everything in her that she hadn't charged into his home, stabbing him with her finger and chiding him at the top of her voice, demanding that he kiss her.

"I'll be just a minute."

Meghan was convinced his mother had told her that as a means of warning her, but as far as Meghan was concerned, a minute was exactly long enough. She waited until the older woman had left the living room and then covered her face with both hands.

"Good heavens, Grey!" she wailed in a thick whisper. "How could you have let me go on that way?"

She wanted to crawl inside a hole, curl up and die. Within a matter of two minutes, she'd given his mother the worst possible impression of herself.

"Meghan, listen..."

She lowered her hands. "I feel like such a fool, barging in here like King Kong. And you let me do it."

"Could I have stopped you?"

She shrugged, then admitted the truth. "Probably not."

"I tried phoning you this morning."

Meghan bit into the corner of her bottom lip. "I know. Mom told me." She could have saved herself a lot of grief had she stayed home a few extra minutes, but she'd wanted to be waiting at her family home when Grey arrived.

"My not coming to dinner had nothing to do with what happened last night," Grey said, reaching for her hand. He reluctantly released it when he heard movement from inside the kitchen. Meghan gave him a reassuring smile; she didn't need his touch when his gaze was so warm and gentle.

"I can just imagine what your mother thinks," she whispered, feeling all the more miserable.

Grey was about to say something more when Frances Carlyle walked into the room, carrying a tray. Grey stood and took it from his mother's hands, setting it on the coffee table.

"Cream or sugar, Meghan?"

"Just plain, thank you," she responded, scooting to the edge of the cushion. There were four cups on the tray, but she didn't give the matter more than a passing thought until Pamela Riverside casually strolled into the room with all the dignity of one who knows she has "arrived." The size of the lump in Meghan's throat doubled in size. She turned her gaze to Grey, and her breath jammed painfully in her lungs.

"When I wasn't home last evening, Mother phoned Dr. Riverside," he said, his gaze holding Meghan's and seeming to plead for understanding.

"Dear Pamela was kind enough to come to the airport on such short notice and drive me to Greyson's house," his mother added in a light, accusing tone.

Meghan noted that Grey's jaw tightened slightly. "I would have been more than happy to come for you myself, Mother, had I known you were arriving."

"It was a surprise, and I hated to ruin it. I suppose it was wrong of me to assume you'd be home, but I couldn't imagine what you'd be doing out the evening before Thanksgiving."

"You were with Ms. O'Day?" Pamela asked, stirring sugar into her tea with a dainty flip of her wrist.

"We were at the movies."

"How quaint." Grey's mother smiled for the first time, but once more Meghan read little amusement or welcome in the other woman's gaze.

"That must have been...fun," Pamela commented, seeming to search for the right word, although she did appear genuinely interested.

If Dr. Riverside was the least bit uncomfortable, it would have been impossible to tell. Actually, there was no reason for her to feel any annoyance, Meghan mused. She was the chosen one, basking under the glow of Frances Carlyle's approval. And who could blame her? Not Meghan.

"What movie did you see?" Pamela pressed.

Meghan should have known that one was coming. She lowered her gaze and mumbled the title, hoping the others wouldn't understand and would let it pass. *"Chainsaw Murder, Part Three."*

Frances Carlyle gasped softly, doing her best to disguise her shock. "I'm sure I misunderstood you."

"It's not as bad as it sounds, Mother," Grey said, and his voice carried a thread of amusement.

"I never dreamed my own son would lower himself to view such rubbish," Frances said, fanning her face a couple of times as though the room had suddenly become too warm. "Naturally, I've heard Hollywood is making those disgusting films, but I certainly didn't think that sort of rubbish would appeal to you, Greyson."

"I'm sure it doesn't," Meghan inserted, automatically defending him. "My brothers were the ones who wanted to see that particular film and they conned Grey into taking them."

"Your brothers 'conned' my son?" Grey's mother echoed, her look all the more aghast. She held on to her cup with both hands and it looked for a split second as though she were going to drop it. The cup wobbled precariously, then steadied.

"I didn't mean it quite like that," Meghan hurried to explain. Every time she opened her mouth, she dug herself deeper into a pit of despair. She cast a pleading look in Grey's direction, wanting to let him know how sorry she was for muddling this entire conversation. "The boys mentioned how much they wanted to go, and Grey, out of the goodness of his heart, volunteered to take them."

"I hardly think that is the type of movie for young boys."

"They're fifteen and thirteen." On this matter, Meghan actually found herself agreeing with Grey's mother. But she couldn't force her tastes on Chad and Danny, who seemed to thrive on horror films of late.

"Meghan's family had invited me over for Thanksgiving dinner," Grey said, directing the comment to his mother. "I phoned earlier and made my excuses."

Frances Carlyle nodded approvingly. "Pamela and I will be preparing our own Thanksgiving dinner," she explained, and smiled fondly at the other woman. "However, it was kind of your parents to invite him, but Greyson's with family now."

From the look Grey's mother cast at Pamela, it was all too apparent that she'd personally handpicked her son's future wife. She'd done everything but verbally announce the fact.

Meghan's heart was so heavy it was a wonder she was able to remain sitting in an upright position. The differences between her and Grey's social position hadn't actually bothered her until that moment. Whenever they were together, Meghan had been swept up in the magic that sparked so spontaneously between them. But it was all too clear that Grey's mother wasn't interested in hearing about magic; she would be far more concerned with passing on the proper genes and balancing out intelligence quotients.

Meghan leaned forward and set her cup back on the tray. She'd barely tasted the tea, but she couldn't endure another minute of this awkward conversation.

"I have to be getting back," she said as calmly as she could. "We're eating earlier this year, because I have to be at work before three."

"What kind of employment involves working on a holiday?" Frances Carlyle asked.

Once more, Meghan had exposed herself without realizing what she was doing. She would have given anything to quietly inform Grey's mother that she was a brain surgeon and was needed for an emergency procedure within the hour. Instead, she calmly announced, "I'm a waitress at Rose's Diner." She didn't bother to look at Grey's mother, knowing the woman's expression would only reveal her disapproval.

"I see," Frances Carlyle said in a tone so like Grey's that it would have been comical if it hadn't hurt so much.

"I'll walk you to your car," Grey insisted.

"That won't be necessary," she said, keeping her voice as even as possible and having trouble doing so.

"Nonsense, Meghan. I'll see you to your car."

Frances Carlyle stood with Meghan and Grey. "There's no need to expose yourself to the cold, son. You can say goodbye to your... friend here."

Certain everyone could see how badly she was trembling, Meghan reached for her purse, buttoned her coat and headed toward the front door.

Ignoring his mother's advice, Grey followed her outside.

"Meghan, I'm sorry," he said, taking her by the shoulders when they reached her car. His eyes were troubled, his expression grim. "I had no idea my mother was planning to fly in at the last minute like this." He frowned and his face darkened momentarily.

"There's no need to apologize. I understand." By some miracle, Meghan was able to force a smile.

"I didn't know anything about this. Apparently Pamela and my mother have been planning this little surprise for the last several weeks."

Meghan would take bets that they'd arranged this about the time Grey had started dating her. She had to give Pamela Riverside credit. Grey's colleague had used the most effective means possible to show Meghan how ill-suited she was to Grey. All the arguments in the universe couldn't have said it more eloquently than those few stilted moments with his mother. Meghan knew that no matter what Grey felt for her, she would never fit into his world. His family had already rejected her with little more than a passing thought.

Meghan had faced this argument before, but always from her own perspective. She'd stood on the other side of the fence, knowing that her family and friends would accept Grey without a moment's hesitation. The one sample of her meeting Grey's colleagues had been slanted in her favor; for the majority of the evening, she'd stayed glued to his side. It was impossible to calculate how the evening had actually gone.

"I'll phone you tomorrow," Grey promised.

"I'm working." She wasn't due in until three, but twenty-four hours wasn't long enough for her to analyze her feelings. If she could delay dealing with this until her head was clear and her mind wasn't clouded with emotions, Meghan knew she would cope better. "When's your mother leaving?"

"Not until Sunday afternoon."

"It probably would be better if you waited until then to contact me, don't you think?" This was Meghan's subtle method of keeping the peace for Grey's sake. She didn't doubt he would get an earful later. His mother was bound to tell him how improper a relationship with Meghan was the minute she drove out of sight. On second thought, Frances Carlyle was intelligent enough to relay the message without ever having to utter a word. She would probably do it in the same manner Pamela Riverside had delivered her own missive to Meghan.

"What my mother thinks or says isn't going to change the way I feel about you," he said tightly.

Meghan loved him so much at that moment that it took every ounce of self-control she possessed not to break down and weep. She raised her fingers and lovingly ran her hand down the side of his face.

"Thank you for that," she said, her voice little more than a broken whisper. She lowered her eyes, fearing that if she looked at him much longer, she wouldn't be able to hold back the emotion straining for release. Her eyes burned and her chest ached.

She started to turn away from him, but his grip on her shoulders tightened and he brought her back against him. Surprised, Meghan raised her gaze to his, only to discover that Grey meant to kiss her. A weak protest rose in her breast, but she wasn't allowed to voice any objection. With infinite tenderness, he settled his mouth firmly over hers. His hands on her shoulders were strong enough to lift her onto the tips of her toes.

Meghan opened her mouth to him, kissing him back with all the longing stored in her heart. She gripped the front of his shirt, bunching the material with her fists, holding on to him as though she never intended to let go. She moaned softly as his mouth moved with tender ferocity over her own until they were leaning against each other.

"Meghan," he whispered, planting a series of soft kisses over her eyes and cheeks. He threaded his fingers through her hair, keeping her close. "I'd rather spend the day with you and your family. I'm sorry it has to be like this.''

"Don't apologize. I understand, Grey.'' She clung to him, her eyes closed. But when she looked up, she happened to notice his mother standing in the picture window, looking out at them. The older woman's face was creased into a look of disapproval so sharp that Meghan could feel its pointedness all the way across the yard. With some effort, she eased herself out of Grey's arms.

He opened her car door for her. "I'll call as soon as I can, but it probably won't be until Sunday afternoon.''

She nodded, and looked away.

"Have a nice Thanksgiving.''

"You, too,'' she said, and slipped inside the car and inserted the key into the ignition.

"Meghan,'' her mother said softly, taking the chair beside her in the kitchen after the Thanksgiving meal was over. "We haven't had to a free moment to talk since you got back from Grey's. Did you two argue?''

"No. He's got company from out of town.''

"You hardly touched your dinner.''

"I guess I wasn't hungry.'' The excuse was weak, but it was the best she could come up with on such short notice. She made a show of looking at her watch. "I suppose I should think about heading off to work.''

"Isn't it a little early yet?''

"I'm sure Sherry's swamped,'' Meghan explained, hoping her mother would accept that rationalization without voicing an objection. "She'll appreciate an extra pair of hands."

"Hey, Meghan," Danny interrupted, strolling into the kitchen, gnawing on a turkey drumstick. "Can you call Grey and tell him we need him for touch football. We're one man shy."

"I already told you he won't be coming today," she replied sharply. She hadn't meant to snap at her brother, but the words had slipped out uncensored before she could put a stop to them.

Danny's eyes rounded and he shrugged expressively, giving her a wounded look. "Well, I'm sorry for livin'. I thought he'd wanta come over, that's all."

"I'm sure he did want to join us," Colleen O'Day assured him, arching a thoughtful brow in Meghan's direction.

Meghan stood, pushing in her chair. Her fingers bit into the cushion on the back of the seat. "I'm sorry, Danny, I didn't mean to jump all over you."

"Will you tell Grey the next time you see him that we missed him?" her brother pressed. "Hey, you're not breaking up with him, are you? Grey's neat. I like him."

"Don't worry about it, all right? What I do is my own business."

"You *are* going to keep dating him, aren't you?" Danny demanded, not satisfied with her answer.

"Who's breaking up with whom?" Brian asked, strolling into the kitchen. Peggy Flynn was with him and the two had been holding hands from the minute she arrived. Meghan had watched them during dinner and marveled at how they'd ever managed to eat.

"Meghan and Grey are on the outs," Danny informed his oldest brother. "He's the best thing that ever happened to her and she's dumping him."

"What?" Brian cried.

"Listen, you two, this isn't any of your business," their mother reminded them. "Whatever happens between Meghan and the professor is their own affair."

"I suppose this means you want us to stay out of it. Right?" Danny asked.

"Exactly," Meghan told him sternly.

"But, Meghan," Danny whined, "where would you ever find anyone as nice as Grey? None of your other boyfriends ever took Chad and me to the movies. I like him. Think about that before you go throwing away the greatest guy in the world."

Unfortunately, it wasn't up to Meghan. Grey's mother would be flying out Sunday. Frances Carlyle had four long days to convince Grey how wrong Meghan would be for him, and how perfectly Pamela Riverside would fit into his life.

If Meghan didn't hear from him Sunday afternoon, she would know exactly how successful his mother had been. It was almost comical when she stopped to think about it. Meghan could have saved Dr. Frances Carlyle a good deal of trouble. She'd already made up her mind about where her relationship with Grey was going.

Nowhere.

Grey lay on his bed, his hands linked behind his head, staring at the ceiling. If he lived to be a hundred and ten he would never forget the look on Meghan's face when she met his mother. She'd marched into his house, insisting he kiss her and God knew he'd been tempted. Then she'd looked around Grey and discovered his mother standing just inside the kitchen, looking at Meghan as though she were the devil incarnate come to corrupt her only child.

Regrettably, Frances Carlyle was no Colleen O'Day. Grey's mother meant well, but he'd long ago given up letting her dictate his life. One of the reasons he'd accepted his position with Friends University in Wichita was in order to escape his mother's constant interference.

For the past three days, Grey had been forced to hear her list Pamela Riverside's fine qualities over and over again until he'd wanted to shout for her to cease and desist. When that ploy didn't seem to be working, his mother had gone on to tell how she prayed she would live long enough to enjoy her grandchildren. This was followed by a short sigh, as if to suggest that her stay on earth was only a matter of time and Grey shouldn't expect her to hang on much longer.

Actually, his mother had missed her calling; she should have been in the theater. And as for grandchildren, Grey sincerely doubted that Frances would want anything to do with his children until they were old enough to conjugate verbs.

Over the course of the same few days, Grey had tried to talk to his mother about Meghan, but every time he mentioned her name, the subject had been subtly changed. Yes, Meghan was "a dear girl"; it was unfortunate she was so..."common."

Grey chuckled in the dark. Meghan common! Dear God, his mother had a good deal to learn about the Irish miss. Meghan O'Day was about as common as green eggs and ham. She was sunshine and laughter, unfathomable, unnerving and incomprehensible. And he was in love with her.

Meghan had been concerned that he would be upset by what Carol and Carrie had whispered in the theater the other night. To be frank, he *had* been troubled at first, but he'd tried not to let it bother him. The age difference between him and Meghan was almost ten years, but it hadn't seemed to affect her. If that was the case, he shouldn't allow it worry him. The one thing that had shaken him more than anything was knowing that his students referred to him as ''Stone Face.'' He smiled. He had a reasonable sense of humor. Now that he'd met Meghan, it was becoming a little more fine-tuned. His students would notice the changes in him soon enough.

The following afternoon, Grey drove his mother to the airport. He did his best not to show his enthusiasm. This visit had been more strained than usual. Frances tried, but she really wasn't much of a mother—the instincts just hadn't been there. Her idea of mothering had to do with manipulation and control. She loved him as much as it was possible for her to care about anyone, and he loved her. She was, after all, responsible for giving him life and for nurturing him to the best of her capabilities.

Frances hugged him close when her flight number was called. ''Keep in touch, Greyson.''

''Yes, Mother,'' he said, and dutifully kissed her on the cheek.

''And please consider what I said. It's time you thought about settling down.''

If he settled down any more, his chest would start sprouting corn, but he kept his thoughts to himself.

"Pamela is a dear, dear girl. I do hope you'll try to arrange some time to get to know her better."

He answered that with a weak smile.

"She's crazy about you, Greyson, and just the type of woman who will help you in your career. Your father, God rest his soul, would be pleased. Marriage can't be taken any too lightly, especially by someone in your position. You need a woman who will give you more than attractive children. You must marry someone your equal." She paused and looked directly into his eyes. "You *do* understand what I'm saying, don't you?"

"Yes, Mother." Grey clenched his hands into fists, battling down the anger that flared to life so readily. He only needed to hold on a little while longer. She would be gone in a matter of minutes.

"Good." Frances Carlyle nodded once, looking pleased that her message had been received. She gave her son a smug look and boarded the airplane.

Grey hurried home. In fact, he could hardly get there fast enough. The minute he was inside the house, he reached for the phone, punching out Meghan's number with an eagerness that had his fingers shaking. He let it ring ten times before he replaced the receiver. Meghan wasn't home.

Chapter Ten

Hello, Eric, it's good to see you again," Meghan
said, draining whatever energy she had by coming up
with a smile. For three nights straight, she hadn't gotten more than four hours' sleep. She was exhausted
mentally, physically and emotionally. Filling his coffee cup, she handed him a menu, then automatically
recited Monday's special—all-you-can-eat spaghetti
and meatballs.

"You look terrible," her college friend commented, studying her through narrowed eyes. "What
happened? Did you just lose your best friend?"

In a manner of speaking, that was exactly what had
happened. Meghan brushed off his concern with a
light laugh. "Don't be silly."

"Meghan, sweetie, I recognize men problems when
I see them. If you need a shoulder to cry on, you come
to Uncle Eric, okay? Or better yet," he said enthusi-

astically, "let me arrange for you to talk to Don Harrison."

"Who?"

"Don Harrison. You met him two weeks ago at the reading group. Actually, Don's interest doesn't lie so much in the classics as it does in you. He's been pumping me with questions about you every day for the last two weeks, but I've discouraged him because I knew you were seeing someone steadily."

Meghan didn't even remember meeting Don, but that wasn't unusual. The reading group had ten faithful members who showed up every week and nearly as many others who came and went as the spirit moved them.

"Listen," Eric continued, undaunted by her apathy. "I'll call Don and let him know you could use some cheering up. He'll be thrilled to hear it."

"I'd rather you didn't," Meghan told him. She just wasn't in the mood to see anyone new. Maybe in a few weeks, when her heart was on the mend; but not now. It was too soon. And she felt too raw and vulnerable.

"Why wouldn't you want to see Don? He'll provide the right kind of therapy to help you get over this guy who's making you so miserable."

It was apparent that Eric wasn't going to listen to her objections, but she was equally persistent and shook her head. She took the pad out of her pocket, hoping Eric would take the hint and order.

"Give it some thought and let me know, all right?"

"Okay," she murmured. But she had no intention of dating this guy.

"Everything will look better in the morning," Eric said confidently. "Just wait and see. Now don't argue with your Uncle Eric, because he's all-wise and he knows all about these things because he's suffered a few broken hearts in his time. By the way, I'll take the spaghetti and meatballs and a piece of the cherry sour-cream pie.''

Rarely had she been more woeful, she realized. It took effort just to get through the day. No one had ever told her that loving someone could be so painful. All her life, she'd grown up believing that when she fell in love there would be birds chirping some sweet song, apple trees blossoming in the distance and enchantment swirling about her like champagne bubbles.

What a farce love had turned out to be.

Meghan didn't even know what she was going to say to Grey. Avoiding him, which she'd succeeded in doing for the last couple of days, wasn't going to work forever. Sooner or later she would have to answer her phone. If she didn't, he would simply arrive unannounced at Rose's, and then she wouldn't be able to escape him.

With that thought in mind, Meghan went on her break. She sat in the employees' lounge and after a few heart-pounding moments of indecision, she picked up the wall phone and slowly, deliberately, dialed Grey's number.

"Meghan, where have you been?" he cried, then promptly sneezed. That outburst was followed by a loud, nasty-sounding cough. "I've been trying to reach you for two solid days."

"I . . . I've been busy. How did your visit with your mother go?"

Grey emitted a short laugh. "About as well as they ever do. I know she went out of her way to intimidate you Thanksgiving morning, but I'm hoping you didn't let anything she said bother you."

"No, not in the least," Meghan lied. Dr. Frances Carlyle had looks that would make a Mafia hit man tremble. In those few minutes she'd spent with her, Meghan had sat with her back straight and her hands neatly folded in her lap. Words she rarely used kept slipping out of her mouth—words and phrases like *indeed*, *quite so* and *most certainly*.

"My mother often means well," Grey continued, "but I refuse to allow her to rule my life. And before you say another word, I didn't have anything to do with Pamela's joining us for dinner that day. I'm not interested in her and never will be. I'm hoping you realize that by now."

"You don't need to worry, Grey. Having Dr. Riverside join you didn't bother me in the least." However, Meghan was willing to wager a month's tips that his mother would convince him Pamela was the woman of his dreams before the year was out. Meghan was all too aware that this ploy to marry Grey off to Pamela hadn't been all his mother's doing. Grey's esteemed associate had done her share—subtly of course, but effectively.

"Good, I—" He stopped abruptly and let loose a series of turbulent sneezes. "Damn, I'm sorry. I can't seem to stop once I get started."

"You sound terrible, Grey." Now that she wasn't so concerned with her own emotional pain, she realized how miserable he seemed to be.

"It's nothing but a nasty cold. I'll be over it in a couple of days, but I think we'd better put Saturday night on hold until we see what this virus is going to do."

Meghan tightened her grip on the telephone receiver. "Saturday night?"

"We've been invited to a dinner party. I mentioned it the other night while we were eating ice cream, remember?"

No, she didn't. Not at first. Then vaguely her memory was stirred. Knowing how nervous she was about attending these formal affairs with him, Grey had offered to let her scoop up the last of his hot fudge topping if she would agree to let him escort her to a holiday dinner party at the home of Dr. Essary. High on her love for Grey and his generosity to her brothers, Meghan had willingly agreed to the exchange. Now she felt like a dimwit. All things considered, the last thing she wanted to do was attend a social function with him.

"Remember?" he coaxed a second time.

"Yes, I guess I do."

Grey coughed and excused himself, returning a moment later. "I'm sure I'll improve before Saturday."

Meghan squeezed her eyes shut as the pain washed over her in swelling waves. "Seeing that you're a little under the weather, and Saturday is up in the air, would you mind terribly if I canceled our date?"

"Meghan, Meghan, Meghan," he chided in a sing-song voice that sounded amazingly like his rendition of *I see*. "You're not going to get out of this dinner party that easily. Honey, the more often you accompany me to these functions, the more relaxed you'll become. I want you with me."

"From the sounds of this virus, you're going to get worse before you get better." Meghan had no idea if that was true or not, but she was grasping at straws.

"That's what I mean about leaving Saturday open. If I am still under the weather, we'll cancel."

"But I'd like to make other plans. I don't want to be left on hold like this," she said, digging to the bottom of the barrel for excuses.

"I don't understand. What do you mean by 'other plans'?"

"I've been asked out by...one of the men from the reading group, and frankly, I'd forgotten all about the dinner party." This was elasticizing the truth to the very limit. But according to Eric, she could have a date with Don Harrison if she wanted one. She didn't. But Grey didn't need to know that. At this point, her only intention was to convince him she didn't want to see him any longer before either of them suffered any more from a dead-end relationship.

"One of the men from the reading group," Grey repeated. He sounded as though he were reeling from this news; his voice was barely audible.

"Since you're not feeling well, anyway, I can't see where it would hurt any to cancel our plans."

"Is it Eric Vogel?"

"No. I already told you, he's engaged."

"I see." He paused, then asked, "And you'd prefer to go out with this other guy?"

"Yes," she whispered, then regrouped her thoughts and stated calmly. "That is, if it isn't too much of a problem for you, since I had committed myself to you first."

A tear slipped out of the corner of Meghan's eye and slid down the side of her face. This was so much more difficult than she'd thought it would be.

The silence that followed was loud enough to break the sound barrier. What felt like sonic booms slammed against her eardrums until her head was shaking and her whole body was trembling in their aftermath.

"I hadn't realized your social calendar was so crowded."

Meghan recognized the anger in his voice and it was like inflicting a wound upon herself. "I'll call you later in the week and see how you're feeling."

"Don't worry about Saturday night. Go ahead and date your friend or any other men you might meet between now and Saturday." His words felt like a cold slap in the face.

"Thank you for understanding. Goodbye, Grey."

He may have bid her farewell, but if he had, Meghan didn't hear him. All she'd heard was another series of sneezes and coughs.

For a full minute after the line had been disconnected, Meghan kept her hand on the receiver. Taking in deep breaths seemed to help the burning pain in her breast, but not much. It didn't help control her need to bury her face in her hands and weep until her soul had been cleansed. But she couldn't do that, of course—not when she had customers waiting.

A violent sneeze ripped the flimsy tissue in half, and Grey automatically reached for another. His head felt as if someone had turned him upside down and all his blood had pooled in his sinuses. His chest hurt even worse; it felt as though a two-ton truck had decided to park there and had no intention of moving. Lord, he was miserable! And he had three classes to get through before he could head home.

Meghan wasn't helping matters any. She'd come up with this cock-and-bull story about wanting to go out with another man Saturday night, and he'd fallen for it hook, line and sinker.

At first.

He'd been so infuriated with her that he was sure the elevation in his temperature had been due to his short conversation with Meghan the day before.

Once he'd settled down, sat back and reflected on their discussion, he realized she'd been lying, and doing a poor job of it. If he hadn't been so irritated with her, he would have easily seen through her deception.

In the light of a fresh day, Grey downright refused to believe she was interested in another man. He couldn't very well claim that at age thirty-four he hadn't been in love before now, but the powerful emotion he felt for Meghan O'Day went far beyond anything in his limited experience. He'd been infatuated, captivated and charmed by any number of women over the years. But it was this one sweet Irish miss who laid claim to his heart. He couldn't love Meghan the way he did and not know when she was making something up.

Grey guessed all this nonsense about her dating someone else related directly to his mother's visit. That aristocratic old lady had buffaloed Meghan into believing she wasn't good enough for him. Grey would bet cold cash on that fact. He couldn't blame Meghan for letting Frances browbeat her into such thinking. Grey's mother had done a good job on Meghan, who'd had no experience in dealing with his manipulating parent. Grey, on the other hand, had had a lifetime of practice; and he wasn't about to let his own mother cheat him out of the best thing that had ever happened to him: Meghan O'Day.

Noticing the time, Grey reached for his tweed jacket, his overcoat and his briefcase. He hesitated long enough to line his jacket pocket with tissues. He was through the worst of this stupid cold—at least that was what he continued to tell himself, but then immediately broke into a series of loud coughs that racked his throat and chest.

"Professor Carlyle, are you all right? Perhaps I should make a doctor's appointment for you."

"Don't worry, I'm fine," he said, waving off his secretary's concern.

"If you're not better in the morning, I really think you should see someone."

The first person who flashed into his mind that he should see was Meghan. A slow smile eased its way across his face. The Milton-quoting waitress would make an excellent nurse—unlike Pamela Riverside, who would probably insist he take cod-liver oil and stay away from her in case he was contagious. Naturally, if Meghan were around, he would have to exaggerate the extent of his sickness. But the mere thought of Meghan sitting at his side, running her cool hands over his fevered brow and whispering sweet nothings in his ear, was far more appealing than a heavy dose of antibiotics or Pamela Riverside.

Before he left the building, Grey turned up the collar of his overcoat. Dear God, it had been cold lately. A fresh batch of snow had thickly carpeted the campus grounds. Several students had taken to building snowmen, and their merriment filled the crisp afternoon air.

Grey heard the sound of Meghan's musical laughter long before he found her in the crowd. A smile teased the corners of his mouth as he paused in the shoveled walkway, holding his briefcase close to his side while his gaze scanned the large group of fun-making young people.

A flash of auburn-colored hair captured his attention and his gaze settled there. It was Meghan, all right. *His* Meghan. Only she was standing with her arms wrapped around another man and her eyes were smiling up at him.

The amusement left Grey's expression to be replaced by a weary kind of pain that struck sharp and deep. It took a moment for him to find his breath. When he did, he held his head high and continued down the pathway as though nothing had happened. He sincerely doubted that Meghan would ever know that he'd seen her.

"Mom!" Meghan cried, flying into the house, her voice filled with alarm. "I need you."

The kitchen door swung open. "Honey, what is it?"

"Grey. He's ill!" She gripped her mother's forearms and swallowed several times before she could continue. Her own heartbeat sounded like a cannon in her ear. "I was on campus earlier and overheard a student comment that Grey hasn't been to school in three days and all his classes have been canceled."

"Aren't you jumping to conclusions?"

"No. When I talked to him Monday night, he sounded like he had a dreadful cold then. Apparently he's much worse now."

Colleen O'Day tucked in a few strands of gray hair behind her ear and casually strolled back into the kitchen where she'd been folding clothes on the round oak table. "I thought you told me you'd decided not to see your professor friend anymore."

"Yes, but he's sick now and—"

Her mother raised her hand as if she were stopping traffic. "Although it was difficult at the time, I bit my tongue, figuring this is your life. You're twenty-four and old enough to be making your own decisions. Whether I happen to agree with you or not, is something else entirely."

"I'm worried about Grey. Surely you can understand that."

Colleen O'Day fluffed out a thick towel and neatly folded it in thirds. "From what you were telling me the other day, you'd decided you didn't much care for the professor anymore."

"Mom," Meghan said with an impatient sigh, "I didn't come here for a lecture."

"Then why are you here?"

"I want you to make your special soup for Grey. I know once he's had some of your broth, he'll feel better. I always did. Remember when I was a little girl how you used to tell me the soup had magical healing powers?"

"Meghan—" Colleen issued her daughter's name on an exasperated sigh and reached for another towel "—how do you expect to get the soup to him? According to what you said, you have no intentions of seeing him again. Do expect leprechauns to deliver it?"

"Don't be silly."

"From what you said, you're not worthy enough to lace that distinguished man's shoes, let alone be seen with him. To hear you tell it, the good name of O'Day is sure to tarnish the professor's reputation and possibly ruin his career. You didn't seem to mind, though, because you'd made up your mind that he was too pompous and dignified for the likes of you anyway."

"You're exaggerating, Mother, and that's not like you. I care enough about Grey to want the best for him. Isn't that what loving someone means?"

Her mother held the laundry basket against her stomach and sadly shook her head. "Perhaps I am stretching the facts a bit, but that's because I disagree with you so strongly. Loving a man often does call for sacrifice, but not the kind you're making. But as I said earlier, it's your life. If you want to break your own heart, far be it for me to stand in your way and gift you with forty-odd years of wisdom.''

Meghan knotted her fists at her side. ''Will you make the soup or not?''

''And who's going to take it to him?''

''You?'' Meghan proposed hopefully.

''Me?'' Her mother laughed at the mere suggestion. ''I'm not traipsing halfway across town to deliver my special healing soup to your old boyfriend, Meghan Katherine O'Day. If you don't care to go out with him any longer, then why should I care if he's ill? He's your friend, not mine.''

''How can you say that?'' Grey had brought her mother flowers, complimented her cooking and gone out of his way to let her know how much he appreciated sharing Sunday meals with them. She couldn't understand her mother's attitude.

Colleen O'Day shrugged as though what happened to Professor Carlyle was of little concern to her. ''All I know is that my daughter wants nothing more to do with the man.''

''He's ill.''

''Why should that bother you?'' Colleen pressed. ''You don't plan to see him again.''

Frustrated, Meghan closed her eyes. ''Will you make the soup, or not?''

''Not.''

Meghan was so shocked, her mouth fell open.

''But I might be persuaded to share the family recipe with my only daughter. It's time she learned of its miraculous healing powers herself. My one wish is that it will loosen a few of her own brain cells so she can see what a terrible mistake she's making.''

The two mason jars were securely tucked inside the shopping bag when Meghan entered the faculty building. Grey's office was on the third floor of the same structure, but that wasn't where she was headed.

When her mother had copied the recipe, Colleen O'Day had done so with the express hope that Meghan would deliver the soup to Grey herself and in the process settle her differences with Grey. Unfortunately Meghan couldn't do that, but she hadn't wanted to disillusion her mother with the truth. She planned to deliver the soup in a roundabout manner and pray that her mother never found out.

Dr. Pamela Riverside would take the soup to him.

After some heavy-duty soul-searching, Meghan had devised a plan of action. She was going to show Pamela Riverside the way to this particular man's heart. It was obvious the poor woman needed help. She might balk now, but someday she would appreciate Meghan's efforts.

As Dr. Riverside's office was on Grey's floor, the same receptionist announced Meghan. Meghan didn't wait, however, but saw herself into Dr. Riverside's room.

Grey's colleague was seated behind a meticulously clean desk in a spotless office that wasn't marked by a single personal item other than her books.

"Ms. O'Day," Pamela greeted, rising to her feet. "This is a pleasant surprise."

But she didn't look pleased, which was just as well. Meghan closed the door and marched forward, not stopping until she stood directly in front of the other woman's desk.

"Do you love him?"

The other woman sucked in her breath. "I beg your pardon."

"Dr. Carlyle! Do you love him?"

"I hardly think my feelings for Greyson Carlyle are any of your business."

"No, I don't suppose you would." Setting the shopping bag on top of the desk, Meghan crossed her arms and battled down an overwhelming sense of sadness. "You're exactly the right kind of woman for him. His mother knows it. You know it. And I know it."

Pamela Riverside cast her gaze downward. "Unfortunately Greyson hasn't seemed to have figured it out yet."

"And he won't with you looking like that."

Pamela slapped her hand against her breast in shock and outrage. "Exactly what are you saying?"

"Your clothes," Meghan cried, waving her hand at the fastidious dark blue suit as though she were a fairy godmother and held the powers of transformation in the tips of her fingers. "I haven't seen you in anything but that same dark suit and jacket in all the times we've met. That thing looks twenty years old."

"I'll have you know I bought this only last month."

"And have five exactly like it hanging in your closet."

Pamela sucked in a tiny breath that told Meghan she'd hit the peg square on the head. "And those horrible shoes have got to go."

With her hands braced against her hips, Grey's associate glared down at her feet. "These are the most comfortable shoes I've ever worn. I refuse to let you—"

"Of course, they're comfortable. That's because your grandmother broke them in for you. Go shopping, Dr. Riverside, throw caution to the wind and try a new department store. Start with a silk teddy and go from there.''

The woman's mouth opened and closed several times, as though she couldn't say everything she wanted to fast enough. ''If you insist upon insulting me, Ms. O'Day, then perhaps you should leave.''

''Take the pins out of your hair.''

''I can't believe I'm hearing you correctly.''

''Your hair,'' Meghan repeated, pointing her finger at the professor, unwilling to brook any argument. ''And do it now.''

With her face growing more pale by the minute, Pamela reached behind her head and released the tightly coiled chignon. The dark length unrolled down her back and she loosened it so that it fell about her face.

The transformation was remarkable. Pleased, Meghan nodded quietly as she studied Pamela's facial features in a fresh light. ''Much better. While you're at the department store make an appointment with a beautician. Have her cut about an inch all the way around, and don't ever wear it up again.''

''Well, I never!'' she barked.

''Well, it's time you did.''

Grey's colleague looked so shocked that she snapped her mouth shut.

''He's sick, you know, and in his weakened condition he'll be more receptive to gestures of concern from you. Go shopping and make sure everything you have on is new. Have your hair done the way I said and then go and visit him. And last but not least, take him this soup and tell him you made it yourself.''

''I rarely cook. Greyson knows that.''

''Lie.''

"Ms. O'Day, I'll have you know I'm as honest as the day is long."

"These are the shortest days of the year, Dr. Riverside. Take advantage of it." Meghan paused and drew in a quivering breath. "Make him happy, or by God, you'll wish you had." With that, she marched out of the office.

Tears brimmed in her eyes, making it almost impossible for her to navigate her way to the elevator.

Grey was on the mend. For the last four days he'd been living on orange juice, canned chicken soup and peanut butter—tasting nothing. The chill that had permeated his bones was gone, but the cough that seemed to convulse his intestines lingered on. He hadn't talked to Meghan in those four days, and it felt like four years. His heart was heavy, his head stuffy and his thoughts more twisted than an old pine tree's limbs. The combination left him in no mood for company, and Pamela Riverside had just phoned claiming she had to talk to him; she possessed urgent information that he must act upon immediately.

Given no choice, he'd changed clothes and put on water for tea, awaiting her arrival with as much enthusiasm as the settlers greeted Indians on the warpath in the 1800s. He would have refused to see Pamela if it weren't for the fact that she sounded highly agitated, which in itself was rare. Whatever was troubling her probably was linked to some problem within the department, and he would prefer to deal with it now instead of on Monday morning.

A car door closing echoed in the distance and Grey braced himself for the inevitable confrontation.

"Hello, Pamela," he said, when he opened the door for her, wondering if she even suspected he wasn't particularly welcoming.

She marched into his living room, her eyes flashing with indignation and her hands knotted into tight fists at her sides. "That woman belongs in jail."

"Calm down," he said, leading her to a chair. Once she was seated, he handed her a cup of freshly brewed tea, adding the cream and sugar he knew she favored.

Waving her hand as though directing a world-class orchestra, Pamela announced, "She pranced right into my office as brazen as can be. I demand that you do something, Greyson."

Grey took the seat across from her, braced his hands on the arms of the chair and dug his fingers into the material, praying for patience. Pamela hadn't so much as asked how he was feeling. It was amazing the things that went through his mind at a time like this.

"Don't you even care?"

Frankly, he didn't. "*Who* pranced into your office as insolent as could be?"

"That . . . girl you've been dating. Meghan O'Something."

Grey couldn't believe his ears. He uncrossed his legs and straightened, digging his fingers deeper into the pads of the leather chair. "Meghan did? Exactly what did she say?"

Pamela's hand went into action a second time. "You're going to love this! She insulted me and threatened me and insisted I lie to you." She said all this in a rush, as though the memory of it were more than she should be asked to bear. When she'd finished, she let a soft cry part from her mouth, then bit down on her lower lip as outrage filled her once again.

"She insulted you?" That didn't sound anything like Meghan, and Grey honestly refused to believe it.

"Yes," Pamela cried. "She made several derogatory statements about my clothes and demanded that I never wear my hair up again. Right in my own office, Greyson. I mean to tell you, I've never been so insulted in my life."

"I see." Grey frowned. He didn't know what was going on in Meghan's loveable, confused mind, but he fully intended to find out.

"I'm sure you *don't* see," Pamela insisted vehemently. Her gaze sharpened all the more. "Something has to be done about this woman.... She belongs in a ... mental ward. I'm still shaking. Just look!" To prove her point, she held out her hand for his inspection, and in fact it was trembling.

"You said Meghan also threatened you."

"Indeed, she did." Tilting her head at a lofty angle, Pamela drew in a short breath as if to suggest she needed something more to calm her before she continued with this tale of horror.

Grey was growing impatient. The more he was with Pamela, the more he realized that she'd attended the same school of dramatics as his mother.

"She claimed that if I didn't make you happy, she'd make damn sure I wished I had. Now I'm not exactly sure what she meant by that, but the whole torrid conversation started out by her demanding answers to what I consider highly personal and confidential questions." She paused long enough to draw in a second quivering breath. "The thing that concerns me most—because it's obvious now more than ever before—is that this ... friend of yours is suffering from some kind of mental flaw, which is probably genetic. Did I tell you that she insisted I lie to you?"

Grey gritted his teeth to keep from defending Meghan, but it was necessary that he hear everything before voicing his thoughts. "Yes," he coaxed, hoping to encourage her to speak freely. "About the lying."

"She delivered some disgusting-looking broth and demanded that I take it to you. What I found most amazing was she wanted me to tell you I'd cooked it up myself. Now you and I both know that while I'm an incredibly talented woman in many areas, my expertise doesn't extend to the kitchen. From everything else this loony woman did, I strongly suspect she could be trying to poison you and then blame me for it. Naturally, the more I thought about the situation, the more plain it became that I had to come straight to you."

"What did you do with the broth?"

"I threw it in the garbage right away. Greyson, it was the only thing to do."

Grey nodded. The soup was a loss, but he was grateful beyond words that Pamela had come to him, although he questioned her purpose. "I'm most appreciative, Pamela."

A smug smile replaced the look of fabricated horror. "Just what do you intend to do about this?"

He tapped his index finger over his lips while mulling over the information. When he'd finished, he straightened and eagerly met Dr. Riverside's gaze.

"I believe I'll marry her."

Chapter Eleven

You want to know what I think?" Meghan asked a group of friends who were sitting in a circle on her living-room carpet. She held up a full glass of cheap wine as if to propose a toast.

"What does Meghan think?" three others chimed in, then held up their glasses, eager to salute her insights.

Tears of mirth rolled down her face and she wiped them aside. This get-together with Eric, his fiancée, Trina Montgomery, and Don Harrison was exactly what she needed to see her through these first difficult days without Grey.

"I think," she said, starting again, trying her best to look somber, "Henry David Thoreau wrote *Walden* when he should have been going for a killing on the stock market." She said this with a straight face, as serious as she'd been the entire evening. Then she ruined everything by loudly hiccuping in a movement so jolting that it nearly dislodged her head. Shocked and embarrassed by the involuntary action, she covered her mouth. Until that moment, she hadn't realized how precariously close she was to being tipsy.

"I bet he made all his students use recycled paper," Trina added, then laughed until the tears streamed down her face.

"Right," Don agreed, nodding. "He missed his calling in life, he should have been a—"

"Boy Scout leader," Meghan supplied.

The others doubled over with laughter as though she'd said the funniest thing in the world.

"I love it," Eric said, slapping the floor several times.

"What I said?" Meghan asked, thinking he might be referring to the continued hiccuping.

Eric and the others were laughing too hard to answer her.

The doorbell chimed and the merriment stopped abruptly. Don glanced toward the door, looking mildly guilty. "Shh," he said, putting his finger over his mouth. "We must be making too much of a racket."

"I don't think we were," Meghan said, doing her best to sober up before going to the door.

Trina covered her mouth with her palm, then lowered it to whisper, "Someone might have called the police."

"What for?" Eric chided. "The worst thing we've done all night is make a few derogatory remarks about Thoreau."

The doorbell chimed a second time.

"I think you'd better answer it," Trina whispered to Meghan. "It's your apartment, and it could be one of the neighbors. Tell them we promise to be quiet."

"Tell whoever it is to lighten up," Don muttered. "It's barely eight o'clock."

Getting to her feet was far more difficult than it should have been. Meghan teetered for a second as the room started to tilt and sway. She walked across the floor and stood in front of her door. Taking in a deep, steadying breath, she smoothed her hair away from her face and squared her shoulders.

"Who is it?" she called out in a friendly voice.

Whoever was on the other side obviously didn't hear because her question was followed by repeated loud knocking.

Startled by the unexpected noise, Meghan's hand flew to her breast. She gasped and jumped back a step.

Immediately Don Harrison leaped to his feet. He was short and a little stocky, but exactly the type of friend Meghan needed right now. She doubted that she would ever feel anything romantic toward him, but he was friendly, patient and kind, and Meghan genuinely like him.

"I'll answer it for you," Don announced, and readjusted the waist band of his pants as if to suggest he was about to walk into the middle of the street with a six-shooter in his hand and gun down anyone who was crazy enough to upset Meghan.

"No...it's all right." Hurriedly she waved off his concern, twisted open the dead bolt and threw open the door. Her gaze collided with a solid male chest. She squinted, greatly relieved that it wasn't the uniform of a policeman that confronted her. Slowly she raised her head, but when she did, her eyes clashed with a pair of deep China-blue ones that were all too familiar.

"What are you doing here?" she demanded.

"Dr. Carlyle," Don exclaimed from behind her. His shock echoed across the room like a cannon firing into the wind.

"He's going to arrest us for what we said about Thoreau," Trina wailed. "I knew something like this was going to happen. I just knew it." She released a small cry and covered her face with a decorative pillow.

"Dr. Carlyle, sir," Eric cried, struggling to come to his feet. "We didn't mean anything by what we said. Honest."

"May I come inside?" Grey asked, ignoring the others and centering his gaze on Meghan.

Had the fate of the free world rested on her response, Meghan couldn't have answered.

The professor's narrowed eyes then surveyed the room, slowly taking in the scene. He focused on each face, finally drawing his gaze back to Meghan. "May I?" he repeated.

"Oh, sure—I guess." Meghan squared her shoulders, then hiccuped despite her frenzied effort to look and act sober.

"Don't let him intimidate you," Don encouraged, placing his arm around Meghan's shoulders.

"I won't," she whispered.

Grey's look swung accusingly back to Don, and the other man immediately dropped his hold on Meghan, retreating several steps under the force of Grey's eyes.

"You're drunk—you all are," Grey announced.

"I'm not," Meghan insisted righteously, then laughed and pointed her index finger toward the ceiling. "Yet."

"I want to know how he heard what we were saying," Eric mumbled, looking confused. "Does he have Superman hearing, or what?"

"I don't want to know how he found out," Trina mumbled from behind the pillow. "Dear God, there goes my quarter grade. I'll never make it out of his class alive."

Don just sat looking dumbstruck and disoriented.

"You need coffee," Grey announced, and moved past all four and into the kitchen.

Meghan lowered herself onto the arm of the chair. Her knees had started to shake and she wasn't sure she could remain upright much longer.

"He walked into your kitchen as if he had every right in the world to do so," Eric interjected, pointing in that direction. "He can't do that, can he?"

"He said we needed coffee," Don reminded the others.

"But how can he walk into a stranger's home and know where everything is and—" Eric stopped abruptly as if a new thought had flashed into his mind. He exchanged knowing looks with Don.

Don was apparently thinking the same way as Eric. His gaze widened considerably. "You wouldn't by chance happen to have met Dr. Carlyle before tonight?" Don asked Meghan, then swallowed convulsively.

"I . . ." Meghan found herself too flustered to talk. "Yes," she admitted in a small, feeble voice.

"He isn't—" Eric glanced toward the kitchen and paled. His Adam's apple worked up and down his throat a couple of times. "No." He shook his head, answering his own question. "It couldn't be."

"What couldn't be?" Trina demanded.

Eric's eyes rounded considerably. "The reason we came over here tonight," he muttered under his breath.

"We came to cheer up Meghan," Trina replied, looking bewildered.

"Because..." Eric prompted.

"Because she was on the outs with her—" Trina stopped hastily, then slowly shook her head. "It couldn't be."

"Did you see the look he gave *me,*" Don whispered. "I'm lucky to be alive."

Eric turned to face Meghan. "Do you know Dr. Carlyle...personally?"

Without meeting his gaze, she nodded.

"Professor Carlyle wouldn't happen to be the guy you've been so upset over, would he?"

Once more Meghan nodded.

"That's it," Trina lamented, wrapping her arms around her middle. "I'm flunking out of college. My dad's going to disinherit me."

"Don't be ridiculous," said Don, looking disgruntled.

Trina ignored him. "My mother will never forgive me for doing this to her. My life is over—and all because I wanted to help the friend of the man who in two months is vowing to love and protect me for the rest of my life."

"Grey isn't going to do anything to you three," Meghan insisted, feeling close to tears. The wine, which had gone to her head earlier, had settled in the pit of her stomach now and she felt wretched. The walls refused to stop moving and she dared not look at the floor for fear it would start pitching and heaving. She was grateful to be sitting down.

"You obviously don't know Professor Carlyle the way we do," Trina whispered, shooting a worried glance over her shoulder as if she expected Grey to return any minute.

"You're taking a class with him?" Meghan asked Trina.

She nodded wildly. "Eric, too."

"I did last year," Don admitted. "All of a sudden I have this sneaky suspicion that he's going to find a way to go back and flunk me."

"You're all being ridiculous," Meghan told them. She hesitated. "Do you want me to get rid of him?"

"No," all three chorused.

"No way," Don said, moving his hands like an umpire declaring a runner home safe.

"That'll only make matters worse," Eric explained.

It looked as if he planned to say more, but he stopped abruptly when Grey entered the room, carrying a tray laden with four mugs of steaming coffee.

Silently Grey passed the cups around, leaving Meghan to the last.

"I haven't been drinking," Eric proclaimed as he lifted the cup from the tray.

Grey paused in front of Eric and glared down at him suspiciously.

"It's true. I was planning to drive home," Eric persisted, his voice high and a little defensive. "I'm just in a fun-loving mood," he offered as a means of explanation.

"It's true," Meghan confirmed softly.

"Is anyone here capable of telling me what was going on when I arrived? I'm particularly interested in your comments about being arrested for what you said about Thoreau."

Meghan noted that the other three were all staring at their coffee as if they expected something to pop up and start floating on the surface.

"Meghan?" Grey coaxed. "Perhaps you could explain."

She swallowed uncomfortably and shrugged. "We were just having some fun."

"Apparently at Thoreau's expense."

"I don't think he'd mind," she said weakly. "He had more of a sense of humor that most educators give him credit for."

"Is that a fact?"

"I mean it, Grey."

"Grey?" Don echoed. He looked at the others and his shoulders moved up and down with a sigh of defeat. "She calls him Grey." This was spoken with such seriousness that Meghan wondered at his meaning.

"Maybe we should just leave," Trina suggested, her voice elevated and hopeful. "It's obvious the professor wants to talk to Meghan alone."

"Yeah," Don seconded. "We should all just leave before—" He let the rest of what he was going to say fade.

"You don't need to worry, I can drive without a problem, ' Eric promised. Before anyone could say anything more, Eric hurried over to Meghan's closet and jerked his coat off the hanger. While he was there, he retrieved both Trina's and Don's jackets.

He was opening the front door before Meghan even had a chance to protest. Now that her head had started to clear, she wasn't sure that being alone with Grey was such a brilliant idea. At least with the others around, there was a protective barrier for her to hide behind.

"I'll see you to the door," Meghan offered.

"There's no need," Grey countered. "I will."

A part of Meghan wanted to cry out and protest that this was her home and these friends were her guests and she would be the one to see them off. But she wasn't feeling particularly strong at the moment, and arguing with Grey now would demand more energy than she was could afford to waste.

Grey seemed to take his time with the task, Meghan mused a couple of minutes later. The four were engaged in a whispered conversation for what seemed an eternity; and although Meghan strained to hear what they were saying, she couldn't make anything out of it but bits and pieces.

All too soon, Grey closed the door and turned around to face her.

Meghan lowered her head so much that the steam from her coffee cup was about to bead against her face.

"Hello, Meghan."

"Hi." Still she didn't look up. "I see that you recovered from your cold."

"Yes, it's mostly gone now."

"That's good news. You sounded miserable the last time we spoke."

"I was, but the cold wasn't responsible for that."

"It wasn't?"

"No."

From the sound of his voice, Meghan knew he was moving closer to her. If there had been any place for her to run and hide, she would gladly have done so. Unfortunately her apartment was tiny, and knowing Grey, he would only follow her.

"The cold was a bear, don't misunderstand me," Grey continued. "But the real reason I was feeling so crummy had to do with you."

"Me?" This came out sounding much like a squeaky door badly in need of oiling. "I'm sure you're mistaken."

"Yes. You, Meghan Katherine O'Day. Plotting so I'd see you making a snowman with your arms wrapped around another man. I'll have you know you nearly had me convinced."

He was so close that all she had to do was look up from her perch on the arm of the chair and meet his gaze, but she was afraid he would read the truth in her eyes if she did. She *had* carefully planned that scene and was shocked that he'd figured it out.

He advanced a step.

Meghan swallowed and, losing her balance, slid backward. A soft gasp escaped her lips as her posterior slithered over the material. She was abruptly halted when her back slammed against the opposite arm of the chair. It was a minor miracle that the coffee didn't end up spilling down her front.

"Are you all right?" Grey asked, clearly alarmed.

It took Meghan a couple of seconds to gather her scattered wits. "I'm fine." Although she made a valiant effort, she couldn't right herself in the chair. Grey pried the coffee cup out of her fingers, and once her hands were freed, she used those for leverage, twisting around so she could sit upright. She did so with all the pomp and ceremony her inebriated condition would allow.

"There," she announced, as if she'd accomplished a feat of Olympic proportions. She brushed her palms together several times, feeling utterly pleased with herself. "Now, what was it you were saying?"

Grey was quiet for so long that she dared to chance a look in his direction. She found him pacing the small area in front of her chair much like a caged animal. He stopped and turned to look at her, then threaded his fingers through his hair in what she thought looked like an outburst of indecision.

"I don't know if this is the best time for this conversation or not," he admitted dryly.

"It's probably not." Meghan was more than willing to delay a confrontation. Her head was spinning, and she was sure it wasn't the wine this time, but the fact that Grey was so close to her. He'd always had this dizzying effect upon her. "You shouldn't even try to talk to me now. You probably haven't noticed, but I happen to be . . . a little tipsy."

"A little!" he shouted. "You're plastered out of your mind."

"That's not entirely true," she protested, just as vehemently. "And if I am, it's all your fault."

"Mine? Where do you come up with that crazy notion?"

That was the last thing Meghan planned to reveal to him. She tilted her head at a regal angle, then pinched her lips together. With a dignified air, she pantomimed locking her mouth closed and stuffing the imaginary key into the front of her bra. Once she'd finished, she realized how silly this must have looked, and decided that if she was ever going to gather her moonstruck wits about her, the time was now.

Her actions seemed to frustrate Grey all the more, and Meghan began to experience a sense of power. She, a lowly waitress, had managed to flap the unflappable Professor Greyson Carlyle.

"All I want to know," he asked with stark impatience, "is why? And then I'll be out of here."

"Why what?"

"Why did you go to Pamela Riverside's office?"

Meghan's head shot up. "She told you?" That much was obvious. Good grief, the woman was said to have a genius IQ, yet she was displaying all the intelligence of a piece of mold. "That's the last thing in the world she should have done."

"Pamela claims you insulted her and threatened her and demanded that she lie to me. Is that right?"

Meghan crossed her legs, then cupped her hands over her knees, praying her look was sophisticated and suave, but knowing it wasn't. "In a manner of speaking, I suppose she's right." If it were in her power now, Meghan would like to have another serious discussion with Grey's associate. It was all too obvious that what the woman lacked in clothes sense she also lacked in common sense. The last thing she should have done was confront Grey and tell him about their tête-à-tête.

"Threatening someone else doesn't sound anything like the warm, generous woman I know."

"Maybe you don't know me so well, after all," Meghan muttered.

"After tonight, I'm beginning to believe that myself."

"Then maybe you should just leave... because as you so kindly pointed out, I'm plastered."

"Maybe I should, but I'm not going to—not until I find out why you'd even approach Pamela... especially when I've gone out of my way to let you know I feel nothing for her."

"She's in love with you."

"She doesn't know the meaning of the word."

"That's not true," Meghan cried, defending the other woman and ignoring the woozy rushes of dizziness that enveloped her. Grey had misjudged Pamela Riverside, and Meghan could understand the other woman's frustration. She remembered all too well how vulnerable his colleague had looked the night Meghan had met her at the cocktail party. Pamela had seen Meghan with Grey and had been devastated. His colleague might have her faults, but she was still a woman and as hungry for love and acceptance as any other female. Strangely, for all her brilliance, Dr. Riverside was shockingly naive when it came to men and the male-female relationship.

"Pamela Riverside possesses all the warmth of a deep freeze," Grey continued, his patience clearly tested. "You can argue with me all you want, but I'm not leaving here until you tell me the reason you found it so necessary to go to her office."

"Because." Her voice was so soft and small. She was certain Grey hadn't been able to hear her, so she repeated herself. "Because." It came out more firmly, but unfortunately it made absolutely no sense.

Grey knelt down in front of her and braced his hands on the overstuffed arms of the chair. "Because? That doesn't tell me much."

"She's perfect for you," Meghan pronounced, not daring to look at him. Although she'd tried several times to push the pain-inducing thought from her mind, Meghan kept imagining what Grey and Pamela's children would look like. All she could envision were dark-haired boys with horn-rimmed glasses, and blue-eyed little girls in two-piece business suits and black tie-up shoes.

"Pamela's perfect for me," Grey repeated and shook his head as if the mere thought brought with it a discordant note. "Honestly, Meghan, if I didn't love you so much, that could be considered an insult."

"An insult!" She'd made the biggest sacrifice of her life for him, and now Grey was calmly telling her that she'd affronted him by gallantly relinquishing him to the woman who was far better suited to his life-style. The unfairness of it all came crashing down on her like a ton of concrete. "I can't believe you'd say that to me. I was so unselfish, so noble and—'' She stopped and jerked her head up. ''What was it you just said? The first part, about . . . loving me?''

Grey's face was so close to her own that his features had blurred. Then Meghan realized that it was the tears in her eyes that had misshapen his visage. Sniffling, she rubbed a hand down her face. His words sobered her faster than ten cups of strong, black coffee.

''I love you, Meghan O'Day.''

''But how can you . . . ? Oh, Grey!'' She leaned forward and pressed her forehead against his while struggling not to cry. ''You can't love me, you just can't.''

''But I do. And I have no intention of ever loving anyone else as long as I live.''

From somewhere deep inside, Meghan found the strength to break away from him. She stiffened her shoulders and rubbed her cheeks dry of any moisture. Her heart felt like a thundering herd of horses galloping inside her chest. ''I'm really sorry to hear that.''

''You love me, too,'' he stated evenly. ''So banish the thoughts of coming up with a bunch of lies to convince me otherwise. I'll refuse to believe you, anyway.''

Meghan blinked several times, her lashes dampening the high arches of her cheeks. She reached out and lovingly traced her fingers down the side of his face. ''I don't think I could lie, even if I tried,'' she whispered. ''Oh, Grey, how could we have let this happen?''

He brushed the wisps of hair away from her cheekbones and his thumbs lingered there as though he couldn't keep from touching her. ''You make it sound as if our falling in love were some great tragedy. From the moment I met you, my life has been better. You're laughter and love and warmth and excitement. I'll always be grateful to have found you.''

"But your mother..."

"You won't be spending the rest of your life with her. I'm the one you're going to be marrying."

"What?" Meghan was convinced she'd misunderstood him. "Who said anything about getting married?" The thought was so baffling to her that she jumped up in the cushion of the chair and pointed an accusing finger at him, waving it several times. "You've lost your mind, Greyson Carlyle."

"Okay, we'll live in sin. But to be honest, that may put my career in jeopardy. Dr. Browning lives by a high moral standard, and frankly, he's not going to approve."

"I can't marry you." She wouldn't have thought it possible, but her heart was pounding faster and faster until it felt like a timed device ready to explode within her breast.

"Meghan," Grey murmured, rising to his feet. "Would you kindly climb down off that chair?"

"I...don't think I should. What would be better is if you left, and then maybe I could think clearly and we could forget you ever suggested...what you just did." She couldn't even say the word.

"Don't be silly. Now, come down from there before you fall." He held out his hand to assist her, but she pretended not to see it.

"Meghan," he cried, clearly exasperated.

"If I step down, you're going to kiss me."

"I'll admit the thought has crossed my mind," he said with a devilish smile.

"And if you do, it'll weaken my defenses."

"As it should."

It took both her hands to brush the hair off her forehead. "I can't let that happen. In fact I think you should leave—you've got me at a distinct disadvantage here. I'm dizzy and weak, and everything you're saying is making me dizzier and weaker."

"I love you."

"See what I mean," she persisted. She slumped back down in the chair, bracing her heel against the edge of the cushion and resting her chin on her bent knees. To her way of thinking—which she had to admit was unclear at the moment—she could hurt Grey's career if they were to marry. "I'm a waitress," she whispered. "Have you forgotten?"

"No, love, I haven't. Are you ashamed of it?"

"No!"

He knelt down in front of her and grinned. His smile carried with it all the warmth of a July sun. "My feelings wouldn't change if you mopped floors for a living. You're honest and proud, and I'm crazy in love with you. I'd consider myself the most fortunate man in the world if you'd honor me by being my wife."

All the resistance seeped out of her like air whooshing out of a balloon. She was crazy in love with him herself, and had been for weeks. He studied her for a long moment, and her reluctant gaze met his. It didn't take long for her to recognize that everything he said was true. He did love and want her, and she would be a fool to even consider turning him away. A smile courted the corners of her mouth even as a tear ran down the side of her face.

Grey reached out and brushed her cheekbone with his cool fingertips. The moment was so tender, so sweet, that Meghan squeezed her eyes shut in an effort to savor these marvelous feelings. Grey was right; she wouldn't be marrying his mother. It would take time and patience, but eventually Frances Carlyle would come to accept her. Meghan couldn't allow their lives to be dictated by someone else. Her mind clouded with fresh objections, but her heart quickly overrode those, guiding her to where she belonged and where she wanted to be—in Grey's arms.

She reached out to him, looping her arms around his neck. He heaved a sigh of relief and crushed her against him, holding her as though he'd snapped her out of the jaws of death.

"Meghan, my love, you've led me on a merry chase."

She wanted to tell him so many things, but she was kept speechless as he rained countless kisses upon her face—moist darts of pleasure upon her flushed features, some burning against her eyelids and others scorching the pulse points in her neck.

"You *are* going to marry me, aren't you?" he asked after a long moment, still kissing her.

"Yes. Oh, Grey, I love you so much."

Grey moaned and returned his mouth to hers, tantalizing her with a series of soft kisses that quickly turned to intense ones that sent her pulse soaring and left her temples thundering. She tangled her fingers in his hair, and arched her body against his.

He kissed her so many times, Meghan felt spineless in his arms. When he buried his face in the soft slope of her neck, they were both trembling.

"I'm not going to let you change your mind," he said on a husky note.

"I have no intention of doing so," she assured him.

Grey paused and reached inside the pocket of his tweed jacket and brought out a jeweler's box. When he lifted the lid, Meghan gasped at the size of the diamond resting between the folds of black velvet.

He removed the ring, reached for her hand, and gazing into her tear-rimmed eyes, he slipped it onto her finger.

With that simple action, the waitress became forever linked with the professor.

Epilogue

"Meghan," Grey called up the stairs from the living room, "hurry or we're going to be late. We should have left five minutes ago."

Squirting on some cologne, Meghan rushed into the bedroom and searched frantically for her dress heels. Grey's side of the room was meticulously organized, while hers was a disaster area. She could hear him moving up the steps to find out what was taking her so long. Angry with herself for not knowing where her shoes had disappeared, she got down on her knees and tossed whatever was on the floor onto the top of the bed.

"Meghan, we're going to be late," Grey said a second time, standing in the doorway. Their nine-month-old son, Kramer, squirmed in his arms, wanting down so he could crawl to Mommy and play her silly game.

"I can't find my white heels," Meghan cried, lifting up the bedspread and peeking underneath.

"Honey, you shouldn't be crawling around down there in your condition," Grey muttered, lowering Kramer to the carpet. Soon all three were on the floor looking for Meghan's shoes.

"I'll have you know you're responsible for my condition," Meghan teased, her gaze locking with his.

"I know." Grey's look caressed her and his hand moved around her waist to pat the gentle swelling of her abdomen. "I worry about you having the two so close."

"It's the way I wanted it," she reminded him. Still kneeling, she turned and looped her arms around his neck and playfully kissed him, darting her tongue in and out of his mouth in a familiar game of cat and mouse, letting her kisses tell him how much she loved and desired him.

"I think we should have waited. Irish twins—I still can't believe it. Kramer born in January and this baby due in December." His hand rested against the sides of her stomach, caressing her there.

Making gurgling noises, Kramer agilely crept between his parents, his headful of bright red curls leading the way. Once he'd maneuvered himself into position, he stood upright, looking around. He hurled his small body against Meghan, laughing as though to tell her he'd won their game. From the moment he was born, he'd been a sweet, happy baby.

"Oh, Kramer," Meghan exclaimed, swinging him into her arms. "You're going to be walking soon, you little rascal."

Kramer squealed with delight as she raised him above her head.

"That's just what we need," Grey said, frowning just a little.

"What?" she asked, busily keeping her son's eager hands out of her hair.

"Kramer walking at ten months. My mother already believes he's a genius, and if he starts walking that early, it will only prove as much in her eyes."

"She surprised me," Meghan admitted thoughtfully. Her mother-in-law had delivered several surprises over the past year, all of them pleasant ones.

"Surprised *you*?" he returned with a short laugh. "You could have bowled me over with a dirty diaper when I realized she was going to be the doting-grandmother type. When Kramer was born, I thought she was going to buy out the toy store."

"Dirty diapers *do* bowl you over," she reminded him, smiling.

He shrugged. "That was just a manner of speech."

"Your mother loves Kramer."

"And you," he said. "She told me not so long ago how you've become much more than a daughter-in-law to her." He paused and rubbed the side of his face. "To hear her tell it, she was the one responsible for getting us together."

"I suppose she's right. Only she used reverse psychology."

"She absolutely insists you get your degree."

"I will, in time—so she needn't worry. But for now, I'm more concerned with raising my family. I've got a year in already and will take more classes when I can."

Grey's eyes brightened and he quickly crawled across the floor, holding up one pair of white high-heeled shoes that were partially hidden behind the dresser. "Here they are."

Kramer crawled after his father, his little knees moving at top speed.

Meghan quickly rose to her feet, slipped on the white shoes and reached down for her son. "This'll be your first wedding, son, so behave," Meghan told him, nuzzling his neck playfully.

"I think it was nice of Pamela to request that we bring Kramer along this afternoon," Grey said.

"He stole her heart, right along with your mother's," Meghan pointed out. "She wouldn't think of excluding him on this important day."

Grey stood, brushing any traces of lint from his pant legs. "Do you think Pamela and Fulton are going to be happy?"

"Yes, I do," Meghan replied, setting her son down and reaching inside her closet for a light coat. "I was the one who was shocked when Pamela came over to tell us she was marrying Dr. Essary. I hope I was able to hide my surprise."

"What I can't figure out is why we didn't realize it sooner. The two of them make the perfect couple, when you stop to think about it."

"What amazes me is how falling in love has changed the two of them. They're completely different people than when I first met them."

"I'm completely different, too," Grey reminded her. "Thanks to one sweet Irish miss who stole my heart and changed the way I view everything from Milton to French toast."

Clinging to the skirt of his mother's dress, Kramer Carlyle struggled into a standing position. Gurgling happily, he looked at his father and took two distinct steps, then promptly fell onto his padded bottom.

"I knew it all along," Meghan said with a happy laugh. She leaned over and picked up her son. "We've got ourselves a little genius."

* * * * *

Silhouette Romance®

AWARD OF EXCELLENCE

LONG, TALL TEXANS

Diana Palmer brings you the second Award of Excellence title

SUTTON'S WAY

In Diana Palmer's bestselling Long, Tall Texans trilogy, you had a mesmerizing glimpse of Quinn Sutton—a mean, lean Wyoming wildcat of a man, with a disposition to match.

Now, in September, Quinn's back with a story of his own. Set in the Wyoming wilderness, he learns a few things about women from snowbound beauty Amanda Callaway—and a lot more about love.

He's a Texan at heart . . . who soon has a Wyoming wedding in mind!

The Award of Excellence is given to one specially selected title per month. Spend September discovering *Sutton's Way* #670 . . . only in Silhouette Romance.

RS670-1R

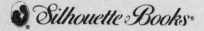